random encounter

Three Player Tag-Team Book 1

allyson lindt

acelette press

contents

1. Adrienne   1
2. Dustin   10
3. Phillip   19
4. Adrienne   27
5. Phillip   42
6. Adrienne   53
7. Dustin   69
8. Adrienne   78
9. Phillip   90
10. Adrienne   99
11. Phillip   108
12. Dustin   118
13. Adrienne   126
14. Phillip   139
15. Dustin   142
16. Adrienne   147
17. Dustin   160
18. Adrienne   167
19. Phillip   172
20. Dustin   181
21. Phillip   190
22. Adrienne   193
23. Dustin   201
24. Phillip   208
25. Adrienne   213
26. Phillip   221
27. Dustin   234
28. Adrienne   246
29. Phillip   254

30. Adrienne   265
31. Dustin   273
32. Adrienne   284
    Epilogue   299

For those of you who are there for all the randomness that falls out of my head and exits through my mouth. You know who you are.

1 /
adrienne

A lot of random things came out of my mouth, some of them at the most awkward times, but I'd never been the person to say *I'd drizzle honey all over him and lick it off.* Or in this case, *them.*

As I sat near the back of the figure drawing class, staring at the evening's two nude models, that was only one of many inappropriate thoughts racing through my mind.

Dial it back, Adrienne.

Not only was the idea not like me, but I was also usually more objective about nudity in a setting like this. I wasn't a student, hadn't been for more than a decade, but I'd gone to college with the current instructor, and she let me *audit* the class and use the room whenever I wanted, so I should at least try to behave.

The Monday night models were supposed to have been a couple in their sixties. I had been looking forward to catching a different type of frame, and at the same time distracting myself. I was starting a new job tomorrow. Basically my dream job, but like if I'd found a magic lamp and the genie had been created specifically to further a porn plot.

I was going to make art for video games. *Score.* A lot of it was going to be erotic art, since the game boasted realistic adult encounters with as many partners as the players wanted. Yup, picture the most popular MMO meets the Playboy Mansion. WOW plus some.

I could handle the nudity part—I wouldn't have gotten the job otherwise—but the sex part? Let's just say a couple of inattentive boyfriends in my past, and an ex-husband who was far more focused on his own pleasure than mine, meant at thirty-seven I didn't have nearly as much experience with sex as I'd like.

When I walked into the class ten minute late, the gorgeous men I found at the front of the room were not the *older couple* I expected. Would asking Scarlet for their names after ruin the fantasy or make it more potent?

These men may or may not be a couple, and they were probably *older* to most of the twenty-somethings in the room, given the silver around the one man's temples. All that just meant I didn't feel like a cougar as I ogled them.

I let my pencil slide over the paper, capturing

the sharp jaw of the one on the right. The shape of his eyes. The clean-shaven chin, and dirty blond hair that just brushed the tops of his ears.

If I let my gaze drift lower, over his well-defined chest, over washboard abs, and to the impressive length dangling between his legs, I'd lose focus and start daydreaming about what other things I could drizzle over him and suck off.

Too late.

I dragged my attention up again.

The other model was just as captivating, with dark hair, a few days of stubble, and broader shoulders.

They both had large bandages on their forearms. Odd, but not enough to obstruct the amazing view.

I bet they'd be even hotter if they were embracing. I wouldn't ask them to just for my art, but I could draw them that way, regardless.

My glances up became fewer and farther in between as I lost myself in the work. In my mind, the blond one was more reserved in public, but didn't hesitate to take the lead in the bedroom. He'd approach the dark-haired man, capture his neck, press their lips and then their bodies together...

The image flowed through my imagination, capturing the sparks of a passionate kiss.

I looked up for another mental snapshot and one of the men had stepped away. The abrupt empty spot on the platform jarred me from my semi-trance. My sketch was rough, barely more than lines, but it was good. What were the odds I could capture this same kind of focus and style tomorrow and going forward?

The woman who hired me must think there was a good chance of me being able to do the job. I needed her confidence—in my skill and in general.

For tonight though, it was time to head home. I closed my sketch pad and put away my pencils. The half-complete fantasies would play themselves out the rest of the way, of blond and brunette making out while I watched, when I got back to my apartment.

I may not have much sexual experience with other people, but I had a drawer full of battery operated boyfriends, and wasn't above picking two to keep me company tonight.

The walk down the art building hallway was familiar. I stepped outside onto a patio with vending machines against one wall, and an assortment of tables and chairs in the middle.

Brunette was seated at one, drinking a soda and wearing a T-shirt and sweat shorts that hugged him just enough to remind me what was underneath.

I'd give him a smile if he looked up, but otherwise, I'd walk right past and be on my way.

"Did you have a good session?" He asked as I drew closer. Damn it, of course he had a sexy voice, too. Deep and smooth, like fingers gliding over skin.

I didn't want to linger and talk, mostly because I was awkward with strangers, and I couldn't imagine magically getting better because this one was hot. My feet carried me toward him without my permission, and I said, "It was one of the better sketches I've gotten in a while. Great models help."

And now I'd stop talking. So far I was doing all right, but no reason to push my luck.

"Glad to hear it." He pushed out the chair next to him with his toe. "Mind if I take a look?"

I clutched my sketch pad closer. I didn't trust input from strangers—they tended to be unpredictable with their feedback. But just as much, I didn't need him seeing my fantasies laid bare on the page.

"I'm not looking to critique or judge. I noticed you were in the zone and I'm wondering what kind of results it produced. I'm a fan of different styles," he said.

I hated telling anyone *no*, but I couldn't tell him *yes*.

"Adrienne," a different male voice called from behind me. *Sean.*

"Oh God, not now," I muttered. What was my asshole of an ex doing here?

Male Model pushed back from the table and stepped up next to me. "Follow my lead."

He wrapped an arm around my waist before I could process. Presumptuous. But it felt good. His light grip on my hip was strong and confident.

Sean reached us. "I was hoping I'd catch you here." As he turned from me to Male Model he frowned. "Who are you?"

"Dustin. I'm Addie's boyfriend."

Addie? No one called me that. It was my full name or nothing. But I liked the way the nickname rolled off his tongue.

"You are?" Dustin asked.

"*Adrienne's* husband."

Not this again. "*Ex*-husband."

"Not until the final paperwork is signed." Sean spoke the simple, infuriating words with all the *take that* I'd come to expect from him.

Paperwork he was supposed to sign six months ago. And one month ago. And last week. We'd been separated more than a year, but I had such a hard time standing up for myself and pushing him to finalize things.

Tonight, with Dustin's arm around me, the pushback was easier. "Great. Sign it and we can move on."

"Not until we talk," Sean said. *Talking* meant him being a manipulative narcissist.

"No."

Sean opened his mouth.

"Look, man, I get it." Dustin talked over him.

"Addie's fucking amazing." He squeezed my hip. "But she's moved on. Do you really want to keep spinning your wheels trying to get to a woman who thinks you're an insecure dick?"

I bit back a snicker.

Sean scowled. "I need to talk to you alone." He yanked my arm so hard I dropped everything.

Dustin grabbed his wrist. "You need to leave." That low, smooth voice developed an edge.

The tension between the men spiked, and my gut dropped. I couldn't move or look away.

Sean jerked away and moved out of arm's reach. "I'll call you later, Adrienne." He turned and walked away before I could come up with a witty retort.

My shoulders sank in relief.

"You okay?" Dustin asked.

I nodded and dropped to my knees by my things, needing a place for my focus while I grasped for composure. Nope, that wasn't happening, because my sketch pad had fallen open to my most recent drawing, and Dustin was naked and kissing his friend, in lightly rendered pencil, on the sidewalk.

I flipped the book shut as he crouched next to me. *Please don't let him have seen that.*

"Really. Are you all right?" he asked again.

The concern warmed me. "I'm shaken, but *just talk to me* isn't new for him. Give a guy a taste of

7

something this incred—" I snapped my jaw shut, because I was joking and he was going to take it wrong and think I was some kind of egomaniac.

"I believe it. I'll walk you to your car and make sure he doesn't stop you again."

I should tell him *no*, but the scenery was nice, he was nicer, and I wasn't up for another confrontation with Sean. "Thank you."

I kept my mouth shut on the stroll, though. I was way too stressed about Sean tracking me down in person to filter my thoughts. "This is me," I said when we reached my car. I could manage that much.

"He's not going to be a problem for you when you leave, is he?" Dustin asked.

Probably not, but maybe. I was nervous now. "I'll head to a friend's first, and make sure he's not following me."

"Stay safe."

I climbed into my car and rolled down the window. "Thank you for your help."

He leaned in close enough for me to see the details in his stubble. "And thank you for the stunningly flattering recreation of my friend and me."

My heart dropped into my stomach.

Dustin turned away before I could find an answer, waving over his shoulder as he walked away. The view didn't diminish my embarrassment, but at least now I was worried about something other than Sean.

The Dustin Embarrassment faded fast. I'd never see him again. Instead, as I left the college grounds and merged onto main roads, my attention alternated between the road and my mirrors far more than I was comfortable.

The next light I stopped at, I dialed my brother, Graham, and put him on speaker.

Sean had always limited his *we need to talks* to email and phone calls. He hadn't sought me out in person without warning before. I didn't like it.

2 /
dustin

Monday evening started strangely enough, with Phillip calling me asking if I was up for helping a friend. I figured he meant moving a couch or something, not nude modeling for a university figure drawing class.

Not that I had an issue with the nudity. I'd worked with the digital version of nude bodies for years, and I was a competition swimmer in high school and college, so I was used to wearing practically nothing for an audience. I didn't have anything to hide.

I also didn't have an issue with the gorgeous woman who had been in the back of the classroom rendering me in a compromising position with my best friend and occasional *more*. I hoped she'd be okay after that confrontation with the guy looking for her. If she'd said the word, I would've decked the guy pursuing her. No one needed that kind of harassment in their lives.

Being her knight in shining armor had my adrenaline racing. Better still, her sketch—that frozen moment in time of sharing a naked kiss with Phillip—was exactly the way I pictured he and I looked when we were wrapped up in each other. The whole thing had my blood roaring with desire. He and I had been so busy with work, like everyone at AcesPlayed, that we weren't seeing anyone. We found stress relief in each other and sex, but it was fast and hard without much time for things like drawn-out kisses.

When I reached the classroom, Phillip was gone from the platform at the front of the room, and the students were wrapping up.

"Did you see where the other guy went?" I asked the woman closest to the door.

She looked up, eyes wide like a deer caught in the headlights. "Next door, I think." Her voice was meek.

So young. Not like Addie, who didn't look *old* by any definition, but held herself with confidence and experience, and had a look that said she'd seen some shit. She was, without question, closer to my own forty than anyone else in this room.

"Thanks." I gave the girl a warm smile, and went to find Phillip.

He was at the back of an empty classroom, head down and focused on the sketch pad in front of him. We were both video game artists, it was how we met, years ago. But we were also old enough we'd learned our craft before digital was a thing. He didn't look up as I approached, his pencil gliding over the paper.

His subject was a woman with long hair falling around the delicate features of her face as she worked on her own drawing.

I wasn't the only one whose attention she caught. An unfamiliar and uncomfortable ping echoed in my chest and I dismissed it. "We're supposed to be the models." I kept my voice low, to not startle him.

Phillip arched an eyebrow. *Fucking sexy.* "She was enthralling. Where'd you get off to?"

"Needed a soda. Ended up rescuing her from a grabby ex." I nodded at his page. "Enthralling and enthralled, based on the way she drew us."

Phillip closed his book. "I assume that was why she was here."

"Not what I meant." I captured his hand and pulled him to his feet, into a similar embrace to the one she'd drawn. It felt good to be pressed against him. "Like this," I murmured before kissing him hard. Maybe we shouldn't do this here, but patience had never been one of my virtues.

He pressed a hand to my throat, shifting the

power dynamic in an instant and controlling the kiss. His mouth was rough and hard against mine. Desperate. Hungry. Or that was me, sinking into and devouring his desire.

This was more like Addie's picture. The fact that she'd conveyed this moment through pencil lines, amplified the heat roaring through me. A sketch and a kiss and I was horny and hard. Neat trick.

Phillip used his full body to push me back to a darker corner of the room. With both of us in sweat shorts, his hardening cock was evident against my hip. We were out of the main view of the door, but voices drifted in from the hallway, and anybody could walk in here.

And now I was harder.

I dragged rough fingers up Phillip's back, pressing closer, grinding my erection into him with the rhythmic pump of my hips. Did I care that I was dry-humping a co-worker in the back of a classroom?

A lot. It was fucking hot.

Phillip grabbed my dick through my sweats and stroked. His rough grip and the burn he left behind was almost too much, but I also couldn't get enough.

"You draw people fucking for a living"—his voice was gravel—"and some random woman sketches us screwing—"

"Kissing intensely. No penises were sheathed in the making—"

Phillip kissed me again, biting my lips and claiming my mouth completely. "We'll have to take this to its logical conclusion then."

"Kissing's logical conclusion is getting off?" I teased.

"It is when clothes start coming off." He stopped stroking me and yanked the waistband of my shorts further down my hips, enough to grab my bare cock and free it. His hands were soft, but his grip was tight and skilled when he grasped my shaft and stroked. He worked me until my hips jerked in time with his rhythm. "I think we should make our own art."

"What did you have in mind?" My voice was barely more than a grunt.

This felt incredible. I didn't know how he did this to me, worked me up then dragged me to the edge of desperation before release, but every fucking time...

"Your lips around my cock is always a pretty picture," Phillip said.

"Dude, inappropriate." I was teasing, and pushing his buttons on purpose. We threw the phrase around at the office all the time. There, it basically meant *back off before HR gets involved*.

Phillip chuckled dryly, and gripped my cock harder. "Fuck you."

"Here? Now? With no lube?"

He pushed me to my knees in response.

I gripped the waistband of his shorts in my teeth and tugged them down, putting me at eye-level with his cock. When I dragged my tongue along the head, he groaned and gripped my hair. I took his length in my mouth, and he bucked against my face.

How was this as incredible now as the first time? It never got old.

Voices drifted closer, and my pulse cranked to *implausible*. I sucked Phillip's cock, bobbing my head up and down as he fucked my face.

My own dick still hung out, aching with need from the attention it just had.

As Phillip gripped my hair harder, I did the same to his shaft, gliding my tongue along the skin, tasting him with enthusiasm.

His familiar grunts, the way they grew shorter, farther apart, told me he was close. When he paused, then jerked inside me with a shudder, I expected the salty spurt that hit the back of my throat.

I swallowed as he came, still licking and sucking, slowing as he did. When he stopped, I pulled away, and he slid from my mouth.

"Fuck." Phillip's voice was raw. He sank to his knees next to me, and grabbed my cock again.

I almost bit back my groan as anticipation surged inside. The whole evening had me so turned on that orgasm built quickly. He knew what he was doing, and I was ready to burst, so it didn't take much to make me come. The sticky mess spurted across his hand, my sweats, and the floor.

"Oops," I said with a dry chuckle.

We both sat there in silence for a moment, catching our breath, listening to the world pass by.

We cleaned up the mess with paper towels from the paint supply room—no reason to leave my DNA over some poor teacher's classroom—and gathered our things.

As we went to leave, I saw Phillip's sketch of Addie still sitting on the desk. I grabbed it to give it back, but for some reason, I tucked it into my own things instead.

The silence between us was familiar and comfortable as we walked to the parking lot. The wet spot on my sweats was a little awkward, but I didn't care. It was worth it.

My phone chirped with a new email, and I grabbed it instinctively.

The email was from our boss, and the contents, the name *Nolan*, made me scowl.

"What is it?" Phillip asked.

I sighed. "Remember I told you about that guy I used to work with, Nolan?"

"The one who claimed you'd stolen his art, and pushed you out of your job over it?"

"Bingo. Apparently, he's claiming AcesPlayed stole his design for their new game." Repeating Judith's message aloud made me even more irritated with the whole thing.

Phillip scowled. "Publicly?"

That would suck worse. We'd come from a company that thrived on public scandal, but here, the game would do that on its own. We didn't need an extra media drama. "Not yet. He's sent a Cease and Desist, and said things will stay between him and Aces if the matter can be resolved quickly."

Phillip dragged out a long breath. "Lovely."

"We've got this." I was annoyed, but the problem was easily resolved. "Everything is in source control. We'll kick the proof over to Legal tomorrow and it'll be fine."

"New person starts tomorrow," Phillip said.

"Perfect chance for them to learn how we make backups and keep histories of all our files, then." I was confident that we'd prove our artwork was our own, and this would go away quickly. I came to work for AcesPlayed because I believed in what they were doing. Not because it was naked people fucking, but it was new, groundbreaking, and a game we were all passionate about.

And I was going to move into the Director of Art position Judith hadn't filled because there were only two of us. I was going to be a part of putting our name in gaming history books, in the most incredible way possible.

But I didn't like that Nolan was back in my life, trying to ride my coattails to glory. Or something. What was his endgame, anyway?

3 /
phillip

I'd reconciled coming home to, waking up in, and overall living in an empty house a long time ago. It wasn't that I didn't own anything, every room was appropriately decorated with *things*. All of them new within the last decade since I didn't want any reminders of my wife. My daughter. The accident that took them from me twelve years ago but left me alive.

The pain had dulled with time, and usually I did a good job of ignoring the memories, but the woman in the classroom last night flipped a switch. It wasn't that she looked like my deceased wife, but their mannerisms were similar. Seeing her so engrossed in her drawing, the way she caught her tongue between her teeth when she was focused, the fact that she was about the same age as Jodie... So much about the woman in class dragged painful memories closer to the surface.

I shook thoughts of the past aside, and rushed my way through a shower, trying and failing to scrub away the gray cloud that lingered over my head. Last night with Dustin was a mistake. I was happy to help Scarlet with her advanced drawing course—I loved knowledge and sharing that with other people—and I rarely regretted the sex when it came to Dustin.

But I needed to be dialing back our friendship, not pretending things were status quo. He was already going to be pissed when he found out what I was up to. When he learned I had an exit strategy to walk away from AcesPlayed.

I dressed and headed down to make breakfast. Coffee. But the dark kitchen was another cloud to the growing storm in my thoughts. There was a place across the street from the office, a gaming cafe that had fantastic coffee and croissants, and a bright, cheery vibe. A stop there meant not staying here any longer this morning.

On the drive, I cranked an 80's hair metal playlist and tried to drown out my thoughts.

They kept trying to drift to the accident anyway. That day twelve years ago when I lost the center of my universe.

Nope. I wasn't getting sucked into grief. Every time I tried to push the thoughts aside, Dustin rushed in to take their place.

He was better than drowning in sorrow. He and

I met when he started working at Rinslet a few years back. They were one of the largest gaming companies in the world and one of their directives was to help shape new talent.

I loved being part of that. Dustin had more experience than most of our artists when he came on, and he was about a decade older. We clicked, we became fast friends, and when this new opportunity came up, we were sucked into the pitch.

AcesPlayed was new. Unique. Zooming toward controversial. Dustin was drawn to the vision of breathing life into this beast he helped create. In fact, despite saying he'd wait until today to work in a rebuttal to last night's C&D email, he was probably up most of the night diving into his strategy.

Seeing Aces succeed drove him in a way I envied. I wished the same things pushed me, but my motivations for signing on were different.

I had hoped that since it was a new company, there would be even more chance for me to help new people grow into their potential. However, given the nature of the game, our hiring requirements were stringent.

Judith—the owner—needed experienced people who could show from their career that they could openly and freely discuss sex without the conversation turning into a harassment nightmare.

I didn't blame her, but it meant I didn't have the same chance to help people learn. She and I had talked about my leaving, and I'd promised to make sure my replacement was trained, if she kept my giving notice quiet until I was ready to make the big announcement.

Even Dustin—especially Dustin—didn't know I had an exit plan.

The new person was starting today. I hadn't met her. This wasn't about friendship. I saw her portfolio, her raw talent, and I knew she had to be the one.

Maybe her starting was what had my mind in this unpleasant place. Not that it was her fault, but her arrival made my decision to leave more real.

Time to accept it.

I parked behind the building where our offices were, and crossed the street to Loading Java. A lot of us made regular stops here. The anime decor was fun, and the staff put up with our intense level of geekiness. We weren't a big enough company to have things like a cafeteria, but in a lot of ways this was better.

Brandon, our Director of Music and Sound, was at a table in front of the shop, scrolling through his phone. Dustin had been a little miffed when Brandon landed a Director position despite being the only person in his department, but like me, Brandon had been around for a while. We'd both been part of Rinslet before it was known as that, and worked with Judith just as long. He had a proven track record, and Dustin was still struggling his way through a reputation he didn't fully deserve.

Brandon looked up when I called his name and waved. "You got a minute?" He asked.

"Yeah. Let me grab something and I'll be right back." I headed inside for a coffee and muffin, then joined him.

He pulled an earbud case from his pocket and handed it to me. "Check this out."

People thought this was odd the first few times he did it to them, but he made a habit of sharing whatever was on his phone, laptop, whatever, so he always carried a second, clean and paired set of buds.

I fitted the pieces in my ears. "Is it a surprise?"

Brandon always shared the most interesting things, from pieces he was composing to random videos of indie bands from all over the world, to the perfect foley effect.

"Yes and no. Danny and Reese being amazing are never a surprise, but this... Just watch." He handed me his phone.

Reese and Danny—Brandon's boyfriend—were Plaid Peanut Butter, a rock band with way more talent than *local band* implied. They dominated a room with their voices and presence.

I hit *Play.* This wasn't one of their stage shows though. The two of them were in the AcesPlayed recording studio, squished closely in the small room.

The music started and I recognized it immediately; it was the theme for our game.

They started singing, sounds rather than words, since the song didn't have lyrics. Mentally, my jaw dropped. Their usual sound was hard and loud. This was a different level of powerful, with her singing stunning soprano, and him coming in with a haunting and complimentary baritone.

I was so captivated, the song ending jarred me. I handed the phone and earbuds back to Brandon. "That's amazing. Are we making a soundtrack change? You have to float this by Dustin, make sure he gets it out there for promo."

"I wish." Brandon shook his head. "This completely breaks their contract, but we were fooling around last night and I had to capture it. I couldn't completely sit on it."

"Don't blame you. Fuck, that's incredible."

Brandon's smile when he said, "Isn't it?" was one-hundred percent smitten.

We continued chatting as we headed back to the office, and went our separate ways when we reached our floor.

The layout was what we called semi-open. In other words, desks went where they fit without having to do additional construction. We were trying to spend smart as a new company, and since several of us had been with other start-ups, we defined that differently than a lot of young companies.

Our spot used to be a satellite campus for the community college, before their business school went largely online. The space was broken into a series of classrooms, complete with the kind of wiring a tech company needed, and each team had claimed one or two of the spots.

There was a tangible tension laced with excitement in the air. We were going into closed beta tomorrow. The game had been announced in professional circles, the public was talking about it, and we'd done closed testing with smaller groups.

But tomorrow, the world would access our game. This thing we'd set off on our own to build, and spent the last few years laboring on in secret.

There was still plenty of work to do. As the art department, our job wouldn't ease up. We'd be designing bonus content, new characters, outfits, levels, gear, position emotes… Absolutely exciting.

Despite the stop, I was early, leaving me enough time to enjoy the coffee and make sure I was caught up on emails and any outstanding issues before the new person arrived.

I wasn't surprised to find Dustin already in the office and working. It didn't matter how many people in the industry painted him as a party boy, he tended toward responsible. He had his shit together and he was good at his job.

The latter bit was partly responsible for the rumors. With such a small company, a lot of us wore different hats, and he'd stepped easily into the secondary role of wining and dining business partners.

Watching Dustin flow seamlessly through the digital history of our artwork, clicking into each place without hesitation, was an experience in skill and beauty. Like most things he did.

I shook the thought aside. I was already too weighed down by people I'd lost, as my wandering thoughts proved this morning, there was no reason to add his name to the list. "You save any of that work for me and the new person?"

He didn't glance up from what he was doing. "There's still plenty to do, don't worry. I want this response to be airtight."

"It will be." I was as certain of that as I was that he was going to be furious when he found out I was leaving the company.

I wasn't looking forward to breaking that news, but I had a couple of weeks while I trained the new person to wean myself from Dustin. That was the best I could do.

4 /
adrienne

Was it wrong that I didn't think I'd been this nervous even on my wedding day?

True, my perception of that day was colored differently now than it had been then, given the way things ended. But as I stood in the main floor lobby of the building where I'd be working, hopefully for a long time, my stomach felt like a rock tumbler.

I didn't have any moral or ethical issues with the fact that I'd be working on an MMO that contained adult themes. I was a lot concerned that I was so inexperienced with the real life version, and that this was my dream job. I couldn't screw this up.

"Hey, sis." Luna's cheerful greeting startled me. She landed next to me and hooked her arm through mine. Her presence tended to chase away doubt, and I needed that today. She was Graham's girl-friend and the reason I even got an interview for this job. "Wave across the street at Violet, and then I'll show you the offices."

So goofy. So fun. I did as prompted, waving across the street at the coffee shop her best friend managed. "Lead the way."

We took the elevator up, and stepped onto the floor where the AcesPlayed offices lived. I'd been here once before for my interview with the owner, Judith, and had the quick tour at that time. Enough to know where the different teams sat.

"Good morning." Luna waved at the man working the reception desk. "Ivan, this is Adrienne, she's our new artist. Adrienne, Ivan."

"Hey." His tone was cheerful. "Luna will show you, but the break room is down that hall. I'm in charge of stocking the coffee, creamer, and stationary supply closet so if you need anything, let me know."

I liked him. "I will. Thanks."

"Tell Daphne we're on our way back," Luna said. "We're taking the scenic route." She led me through the hallways, pointing out the doors for QA, Development, Music, Writing... We didn't interrupt because there were people working already. Also, there was no way I'd remember every-one's names if I had to absorb them at once.

As we neared the Art room, I swore I heard a familiar voice, but I couldn't place it. For all I knew,

I'd overheard someone on campus one day who sounded similar.

"And this is lonely little me." Luna stopped in front of an office at the end of the hall. "I'm told I can have minions in a few months, but for now, it's just me. Which means you can come visit whenever you want and we won't be disturbing anyone else."

"Noted," I said with a grin.

She knocked on the open door next to hers, and introduced me to the head of HR, Daphne.

This part of a new job was the same no matter where I went. I spent the next hour filling out paperwork and reading through company policy. When I was done, Daphne took me to meet my new co-workers.

As we strolled toward the Art room, the door was open this time.

"Top five things you leave behind in a zombie apocalypse. And go." The voice that drifted into the hallway was deep, teasing, and super sexy. Probably not the safest thing to be thinking as I met the men who I'd be drawing sexy cartoons with.

"Oh. Um... My stash of solid gold bars."

My step faltered. I knew that voice for certain. I'd heard it last night.

Daphne glanced at me. "Are you all right? I can ask them not to do that."

"No, it's fine." I didn't have a problem with the

conversation. "First day nerves." That couldn't be Dustin.

We stepped into the room as the other voice said, "Gold can be melted down. Used."

"But there are far more valuable materials that weigh far less." Oh, God, it really was him, and he hadn't looked up yet.

And his equally gorgeous, currently clothed friend. "Okay, let's say you own such a thing. That's one."

Sitting casually in my new workspace, looking and sounding like this was their domain and everyone knew it, were the nude models from last night. The two men I'd fantasized about screwing each other, and at least one of them knew what I'd been drawing.

"*Addie.*" Dustin grinned when they finally saw me. "You're the new talent? No shit. That's awesome."

"It's Adrienne," Daphne corrected him with a smile that didn't reach her eyes. "You all know each other?"

I wouldn't correct the nickname, one because I liked it, and two because I hated telling people *you're wrong.*

"Yes, but no," Dustin said. "We met last night."

Please God, don't let him say where or why.

The other man extended his hand. "I'm Phillip. It's great to have you here."

"Thanks. I'm excited to be here." They weren't making a big deal out of things. Yet. I could pretend this was all perfectly normal. I'd do that until I was required to do otherwise anyway.

"Adrienne, you know where to find me if you need anything," Daphne said. "Please keep in mind, our rules aren't lip service. Not that I expect these two to give you any issues."

"Thank you."

Phillip pointed me toward my desk, which had the most amazing setup of three giant screens and a high end computer plus drawing tablet that I'd ever seen. He told me my password was on a post-it on the screen and to change it immediately.

When I logged in, he pointed me toward some internal graphic assets and told me to get familiar with the setup, and ask him if I needed anything.

"I'll do that, thank you." So far, so good.

"And to address the elephant in the room..." Phillip said.

No. We didn't have to do this, did we? We could just pretend last night was other people? "Okay?"

"I'm glad you're continuing to hone your skills, like with last night's class. I'm a big supporter of that."

"I'm glad to hear it, since I'm not the real Adrienne. The view last night was so breathtaking, I kidnapped your real new employee and took her place." I mentally facepalmed even as the words tumbled past my lips. What was wrong with me? "I'm kidding, of course. I'm sorry, I didn't mean..." What? I meant exactly what I'd said, but in a joking way. Not in an *I'm here to stare at you because you're sexy naked* kind of way.

"Good. Because we can't condone kidnapping." Phillip's tone was serious and his expression blank.

Dustin looked like he was fighting a smirk. "It's understandable, though. We *are* gorgeously irresistible."

One corner of Phillip's mouth twitched up, cracking his mask. "That's a fact. And you won't work with two better artists in the industry."

False bravado was a turn-off, but genuine confidence was fucking sexy, and I'd seen art samples coming out of this group, so I knew they were incredible at what they did. Still, I'd swooned enough. I should at least try to play it cool. "Is that so?"

"We're *highly* recruited." Dustin straddled his chair and rested his arms on the back. The pose elongated his toned arms and back, and stretched his T-shirt over lines of definition. *Drool.* It also tugged up his sleeve, revealing the bottom of a tattoo I recognized immediately. Luna had a similar one of the AcesPlayed logo. That was what they'd been hiding with the oversized bandages last night.

Phillip nodded "But we'll make you one of us. You've got the skill."

"You just need the right connections," Dustin said.

Watching the back and forth, the way they played off each other, was fun. No wonder they looked so good in that embrace last night. "Wait. Are you together? You have to be." Damn it, why couldn't I keep my mouth shut? Because I was nervous. Lousy excuse, but the only one I had.

Phillip shrugged. "Co-workers. Just like you."

"Also friends and fuck-buddies," Dustin added.

He said it so nonchalantly and Phillip didn't even flinch. Fuck-buddies. As in casual sex? I knew people did that, but I had a hard enough time finding relationship-sex. I couldn't fathom liking someone well enough to just sleep with them then hang out the next day, though the idea was appealing. I certainly didn't care for relationships right now. Maybe I could learn? Maybe one of them could teach me?

Definitely inappropriate, and I needed to change the subject before the thought forced its way past my lips. "So you're saying who I know is more important than talent?" I could take us back to our previous topic. "In other words, your being highly recruited doesn't mean anything."

"Talent and making sure it's recognized mean everything." Phillip pulled up a seat and rolled closer. "Knowing people makes the rest easier."

"And after last night, you know more about us than a lot of people." Dustin winked.

Phillip smirked. "Don't let him fool you, a lot of people know that side of him."

If they were going to treat the art class like this, teasing but not embarrassing me, I could deal with that. Especially since they let me move on so easily from my question about their relationship. "But how many of them noticed that birthmark?"

"I doubt very many." Dustin glanced at the computer screen behind him. "Shit, I need to run to a meeting. If you do any more in-person figure drawing, wait until I'm back." A hint of seduction slid into his voice.

"Dude. Inappropriate."

Phillip's retort surprised me. The entire conversation was probably inappropriate. But the fact that we drew sex meant a lot of lines weren't clear to me. "Isn't that exactly what we do here?" I was supposed to watch out for language that made me uncomfortable, but I didn't feel threatened by the conversation. Maybe it was because it didn't take me much to summon fantasies of them fucking.

"The lady is correct," Dustin said. "That's exactly what we do here."

"Uh-huh." Phillip managed to convey *you know what I meant*, but still keep it light, in a simple grunt.

"Before I go"—Dustin focused on me—"I'm glad you're here, Addie. Can I call you that?"

"Yes." It was okay that my gorgeous new co-worker had already given me a nickname. It didn't mean anything. Why would I even think it did? Ridiculous.

"Perfect." Dustin turned to Phillip. "I'm also leaving behind the TV remote, my wireless stereo setup, my credit cards, and my bottle cap collection."

Phillip laughed. "You'll never be able to pay for things if you leave the bottle caps behind."

"I'll sell my body. It's my best commodity anyway. Catch you in a few, Addie." And with that, Dustin was gone.

Phillip wheeled his chair to sit next to me. "When he gets back, he can fill us in if he needs any help with what he's working on, but until then, are you ready to get started?"

"Sure." As long as diving into work distracted me from daydreaming about Phillip and Dustin.

"Most of what we use was designed in house— well, Rinslet's house—but it's structured like what you're already familiar with. There's a document on your desktop with network paths." When Phillip gestured at the screen, he leaned in, and I caught the faint scent of a musky cologne.

Gorgeous, skilled, and he smelled incredible. God help me I was going to spend half my work days distracted if I didn't learn how to relegate these two to plain, boring co-workers.

"We have a company meeting in an hour," Phillip said. "Spend the time before then exploring assets and getting familiar with the software. Let me know if you have any questions. After the kick-off, we can go more in depth."

Yes, sir. Bad Adrienne. "Sounds good. Will do."

"You'll be great." Phillip squeezed my shoulder and desire whispered through me.

As he rolled back to his own desk, I forced myself to focus on my work. It was easier than I expected to lose myself in exploring this new, amazing environment. Part of me kept chanting *I can't believe it. I'm really here.*

I lost myself in the work deeply enough that when my calendar chimed with a reminder, it took me a moment to register.

"May I escort you to the large conference room?" Phillip asked.

I smiled at the exaggerated formality, stood, and gave him a short curtsy. "I'd be honored." Where did that come from? I wasn't that laid back person. Would he think I was a dork?

His chuckle rolled over me like skilled fingers dancing along the shell of my ear. "You're going to fit in great here. Let's go."

As we headed toward a part of the floor I hadn't been to yet, Luna fell into step with us. "Are you being nice to my sister-friend-wife-in-law?"

Phillip glanced at her with a raised eyebrow. "I

think that sounds very different than what you mean."

"Does it?" Luna stared back with feigned innocence. She turned to me. "He didn't answer the question. They're not hazing you, are they?"

"No. Is that a thing here? Will I have to run naked through the halls to prove my loyalty?" Damn it, that was inappropriate.

"Of course not." Phillip sounded scandalized. "We limit it to public flogging, and only if you beg."

Images flashed through my head of me naked and on display, Phillip drawing a leather flogger lightly across my ass, and then with more impact. I swallowed a whimper.

"Dude." Luna elbowed him, her tone light. "Inappropriate."

Oh, right. If he weren't doing wicked things to my thoughts, would the comment be acceptable? "It's okay," I muttered, meaning more by the simple phrase than my generic brush-off implied.

We reached a large room with a stage up front, that was probably a lecture hall at one point. Rows of chairs set up near the front of the room. Groups of two to five people clustered together, rings of empty chairs around them.

"They're not as cliquey as they look," Luna said. "Everyone's on deadline, so they're probably going to whisper during parts of the presentation."

Phillip coughed.

Luna shrugged. "You do the same to them."

"*I* don't," Phillip said.

I didn't quite understand the dynamic here. In any of the company. Expected, but that didn't stop me from wanting to figure it out sooner rather than later. More perplexing though, I couldn't figure out Phillip. I wasn't used to being unable to read people at all.

We sat in the front row. Not that there were enough rows for there to be a big difference.

Dustin stepped to the front of the room with the confidence of a man who was comfortable taking his clothes off for a class of artists. "I won't subject you to the same crowd-working that we've all seen too many times, but I do want to see a little excitement. We're here. We're finally going live with this thing we've built. Who's excited?" His tone was coaxing and energetic.

It was almost enough to make me *whoop* and I didn't have the same kind of investment in this as everyone else here. Luna, Phillip, and one other person let out loud enough cheers to almost make up for the lack of response from anyone else.

Dustin didn't look fazed. "I'll take it. Before we dive in, since most of you apparently aren't excited" —his tone was light and teasing—"new face in the house is Adrienne. She's ours, so hands off."

Did I just turn a hundred shades of red?

"We specifically have a *don't stand up and tell*

everyone about yourself policy, so if you want to know about her, be a normal person and introduce yourself later," Dustin said.

I breathed a sigh of relief and light laughter rippled through everyone.

"In case no one has noticed, it's hard to keep a secret in an office like ours. Because of that, I won't delve into all the hot new merchandising that's coming, or the clan details, or anything you already all know." Dustin rolled with this as naturally as taking a breath, and he was amazing to watch. Though, my teasing memories of what lay under the clothing may be adding to my fascination.

His pause lasted longer than I expected, though. The room had gone still, and all eyes were on him.

The room went dark. A chorus of gasps and murmurs erupted around me. It wasn't a power outage, light still seeped in from the hallway.

Phillip leaned closer. "Wait for it," his voice was barely a whisper.

"I *will* get you to show excitement about this." Dustin's voice carried through the darkness. A dim glow grew behind him slowly enough that my eyes adjusted along with it, and the company logo appeared on a screen on the wall, back-lighting Dustin.

"We're not a bunch of fanboys at E3," a friendly call came from the audience. "Is the drama necessary?"

Dustin pointed in his general direction. "I'm glad you asked. It's called hype, and yes, we absolutely cannot announce this without it."

"That's Elliot," Phillip said. "He's one of the developers, and while he's grumbling now, he'll be an early and long-term adopter when he sees this."

"There's a typo in your *Introduces*," someone else said.

Dustin didn't so much as flinch toward the screen. "No, there's not."

"That's Nigel. Quality Assurance," Phillip said quietly.

"AKA, the jerk squad."

I'd never heard that kind of disdain from Luna. How bad were they?

Phillip *tsk*ed. "Everyone's here because we like each other and we're the best at our jobs. Sometimes personalities clash, but they don't mean anything by it."

Luna scowled. "Whatever."

"When beta kicks off tomorrow, and over the next few weeks and months, most of us will be in game at least a little bit. And don't pretend you won't all be lurking in the forums." Dustin's confidence and stance never wavered, despite the ribbing. "And we're going in there to present a united front, despite our different clans, as the AcesPlayed team."

The screen changed, the new slides showing rows of illustrations, each with a name underneath and one of four symbols—a diamond, a heart, a club, or a spade. I recognized Dustin, Phillip, and Luna in the images, and the others matched the faces of the other people in the room.

Luna clapped and whistled. "If you don't think that's cool, there's something wrong with you," she said loud enough for the room to hear. "Did you guys draw those?"

Dustin grinned. "Every single one. Happy game birthday, all."

Everyone applauded and my eyes swept the screen, trying to associate at least a few names with faces. It wouldn't stick, but it might help me remember more easily when I was introduced to each of them. My breath caught in my throat when I landed on my avatar next to Phillip's.

It was a pencil sketch instead of a full-color painting like the others. "How..." Or rather when did he have time?

"They have you too." Luna hummed with excitement.

"We'll shift it to a full color one later, but we wanted to make sure you were up there with the team." The smooth, lightheartedness had vanished from Phillip's voice, and was replaced with something heavier.

What had I missed?

5 /
phillip

I recognized the sketch of Adrienne in the employee line-up because it was mine. From last night. I thought I'd tucked that away, buried it in my sketchbook to take home and pretend the stranger in the back of the classroom didn't summon intense memories of my past.

Seeing Adrienne's surprise and glee at being included already pushed away any hints of frustration, but didn't erase the tug of guilt and grief.

I kept half an ear on Dustin's presentation as he rolled through the rest of the news. It wasn't that I was bored, but he'd done a dry run with me for timing—he always did—and I knew what he was going to say.

My focus was on Adrienne, though. As the meeting progressed, her shoulders relaxed, the smile tugging up the corner of her lips lingered longer each time, and she rarely took her attention off Dustin.

There was something there. Maybe not a long term attraction, it was too early to tell, but definitely a fascination that ran both ways and would probably become a deeper friendship. The longer I watched her, the easier it was to separate her from the memories she'd triggered. She had a lot of mannerisms in common with Jodie, but Adrienne was starkly and beautifully her own person.

And she had already proven she clicked with Dustin. Good. That would make it easier when I left. Judith was rarely wrong about team dynamics, and I was glad I'd let her make this decision. Regardless of what the disagreement in the back of my mind was whispering.

The meeting wrapped up and Adrienne, Luna, and I headed back to our offices, Luna breaking off when we reached the Art room.

"But seriously," Adrienne said, resting a hand on the back of her chair instead of sitting. "How did Dustin pull off that sketch of me? You probably don't know. I thought he was in a meeting."

"I was." Dustin joined us. "Besides, I'm more of a charcoal and oil pastels kind of guy. Phillip did it."

I was grateful his answer glossed over other details. "I'll finish it up for you today." I told her. "So if you see me staring at you, don't think anything of it."

"You make it sound easy." Pink dotted her cheeks and crept down her neck.

I bet her breasts flushed as well. I wouldn't mind the chance for a little role reversal from last night, where I got to use her and Dustin as models. That thought would wait for more exploration later.

"My part *is* easy. Great view, appreciative subject..." I needed to dial it back. I was rarely in the mood for a serious *Dude, inappropriate.*

"Judith probably explained this to you, since it's part of her on-boarding pitch, but a lot of the people here, including Phillip, came from Cord before it was Rinslet. The company culture was, as I understand it, *different,*" Dustin said.

Different. I was amused at his vagueness. Dustin had never had a problem with the casual sex between co-workers, but he also continuously seemed skeptical that in our early days, as young, dumb, full of cum gamers, we'd turned our job into one big after party of orgies.

Adrienne laughed through the blush. "Different? That's one way to put it. God, the stories I've refused to listen to about just how many tabs can fill slots during a launch celebration."

She knew Cole. Most of our new hires were referrals—who someone knew did matter here, mostly because it made it easier to gauge if they'd be a good fit in this environment. "Adrienne is Luna's other boyfriend's sister," I explained.

"Wow." Adrienne's lips formed a perfect *O*. "That was almost more convoluted than sister-friend-wife-in-law."

"Wait. You know The Wizard." Dustin met Cole once, and was fascinated with him. Or maybe not with Cole so much as his history. He was a jack of all trades at Rinslet, Judith's ex-husband, and one of the few people we knew who'd walked away from the gaming industry almost completely.

Adrienne raised her eyebrows. "It's my understanding, from him, that no one called him The Wizard."

"Only Judith." It all seemed like so long ago, and at the same time, some of those memories were still fresh. I mentally cleared my throat to kick myself back on track. "Dustin's point is, I'm sure"—to distract Adrienne from asking when I sketched her—"if I, or anyone, gets to be too much…"

"I know. If I see something, say something. So far, I'm good," Adrienne said.

I liked her. She was going to fit in great here. "Back to work. You've had all of a morning to be overwhelmed, but do you have any questions so far? About anything?"

"I'm sure I do. But right now, I don't know what I don't know. Um… *Oh*." Her face lit up. "What are your five things?"

She meant the game she'd walked in on between me and Dustin. My mind blanked as I reached for an answer that didn't sound as cold as the truth. "What?" Not my best comeback ever.

"Dustin said people should talk to me if they wanted to get to know me. Goes both ways, doesn't it? Your five things you'd leave behind in a zombie apocalypse."

"It's just a game we play. Prompt changes every time." Still not a great answer. Why did this one thing knock me off balance? Because the answer was *I could leave it* all *behind*, and she'd take that wrong.

"Let's get lunch." Dustin's changing the subject was neither smooth nor subtle, but I was grateful for it.

Adrienne furrowed her brow. "It's not even eleven thirty."

"True. But the best places fill up at noon, so we want a table early, and it's your first day, so we might be there a while, making sure we're a cohesive team," Dustin said. "What do you like? Chinese? Italian? Mexican? Indian?"

Adrienne shrugged. "How boring am I that I'm always on the prowl for the perfect sandwich?"

I've got your perfect sandwich right here. You, between the two of us. Nope. This was now, not fifteen years ago, and telling the new employee she'd look even tastier stuffed from both sides was most definitely inappropriate.

"There's a great place about two blocks down. We'll walk, enjoy the sunshine, and talk about what you were doing in that classroom last night." I shouldn't bring that up again, she'd looked embarrassed enough the first time, but I was genuinely curious and I wanted to make sure the topic ceased being taboo.

Adrienne grabbed her purse. "Fine. But you owe me the same in return. I've seen your dicks, you can at least tell me why they were hanging out. Actual answer on this one." She winced and covered her face with her hand, peeking out between her fingers after a heartbeat. "I mean... I didn't mean however that sounded. Please don't take that wrong."

I *really* liked her. "I won't. Just this once."

"You'd better leave it an open-ended offer." She finally lowered her hand. "It's going to happen a lot."

"So let it." I jerked my thumb toward the elevator. "Last night. Spill."

The three of us stepped into a waiting lift. "If you're looking for lurid or interesting, you won't get it from me," Adrienne said. "Scarlet Barton knew my brother when he worked at the university, and introduced me. Creating at home hasn't always been the easiest, so she lets me use a studio whenever I want, and sit in on any classes I'm interested in."

Dustin turned to face us, back to the doors, as we rode down. "Including the naked ones."

"Figure drawing is part of the curriculum, and I like drawing figures." Adrienne's tone was casual with a hitch.

Dustin ginned. "So I saw."

"Once again, I'm not the one who was naked." The longer she talked, the less hesitant Adrienne sounded.

"And I'm not the one who was embarrassed." Dustin stepped backwards off the elevator, not looking until all of us had cleared the doors.

I wasn't letting his throw-away comment turn things stilted and awkward again. "Scarlet and I go way back. We were in graduate school together. She called me last night, said she had a last-minute cancellation and did I know anyone? It sounded like fun, so I volunteered us."

We stepped outside, and the sun caught the golden highlights in Adrienne's light brown hair. As if they'd planned it, she and Dustin both paused and turned their faces toward the heat, their eyes closed.

Stunning.

"Let me make sure I understand—a friend calls, says *I need someone to take their clothes off for a classroom full of college students*, and your first reaction is *I'm in*." Adrienne's voice was calm. She finally opened her eyes again and met my gaze.

I shrugged. "Yup."

She looked at Dustin. "And you were just like *okay, dude, let's go.*"

"I've seen him naked before. I was pretty sure my lust was sated enough to control myself for an hour or two."

Not any longer than that, but I wasn't complaining about the way last night ended.

"Right. Co-workers, friends, and fuck-buddies." Adrienne sounded skeptical. "And I'm not quite sure I understand how easy it was for either of you to sign on, but I see other people do it all the time, so I'll stop projecting my insecurities on you."

We headed toward the sandwich place, and the sounds of downtown traffic filled in the lull in the conversation.

Dustin started to whistle, most likely whatever he'd heard last on his playlist of the week. It was something he did when he was relaxed and unfocused, and it was always nice to hear.

"I never got the hang of whistling," Adrienne said. "Not sure if it's the putting my lips together part or the blowing part." Her step faltered.

"Only one way to find out," I said before she could take it back.

"Practice makes perfect." Dustin didn't miss a beat.

The bright red on Adrienne's cheeks was exaggerated in the sunshine, but it looked good on her.

"Do *not* encourage the random outbursts. I'm bad enough as it is. The number of times I've been told I seriously need help."

"You seriously need to not worry about it." I hated it when people filtered their thoughts. If this was Adrienne uncut, good. "I already told you, it's not a problem."

"I will help you with the whistling, though. Come here." Dustin stepped in front of Adrienne, stopping them both.

I paused as well, curious.

"Make a tight circle with your mouth." Dustin dragged a thumb over Adrienne's bottom lip.

Her sharp intake of breath matched mine. Such an alluring sight.

"There's your problem." Dustin smirked. "*Blowing* means the air goes out, not in." He whistled again, a light and carefree melody.

Adrienne blew out a puff of air, which sounded exactly like that—a puff of air.

"Your tongue needs to work with your teeth and lips." Dustin nudged her shoulder lightly with his own, and we were all walking again.

"I thought teeth were a big no-no with blowing." Adrienne winced.

Smart woman. "I'm with her on this," I said.

Dustin sighed. "*For whistling*. I work with a pair of fucking perverts."

"Takes one to know one." I couldn't argue the observation.

"I may be inexperienced, but I'm seeing a distinct lack of fucking." This time Adrienne barely flinched.

Good.

"Left it back at the office. Don't worry, you'll get your fill."

I could take Dustin's words so many ways. But there was a line between innuendo and outright descriptions of the sex we'd had, and I should steer clear of the latter. Probably. Maybe. "Have you?"

"Gotten my fill? As in... physically or is this more of a psychological thing?" Dustin asked.

"Unless those renderings come to life, I'm guessing not physical." Adrienne plucked a loose leaf that had landed in a nearby bush and rolled the stem between her fingers. "And tangent, but orcs are not nearly as well hung as I expected."

And I'd made them that way on purpose. If someone wanted to play the big guy, they didn't get a huge cock for it. "It's all the muscle mass. Makes a dick look smaller."

She glanced at me, disbelief sprawled across her face. "*Right.* I can hear it now. *I don't have a tiny penis. I just work out a lot.*" She spoke in a false baritone.

Dustin and I laughed.

She'd been here half a day and she already fit so

well. I couldn't have gotten luckier in finding a replacement.

And the longer she was around, the better she slid into the culture, the less the pit inside over leaving would bother me.

6 /
adrienne

When I got to work Wednesday morning, the Art room was empty. I glanced at my phone clock, and then at my computer clock, as I got logged into my machine and checked my email. Empty, of course. It was odd being so new at a job that no big tasks waited for me. I was excited for when that was no longer the case. It was a few minutes before eight thirty, but yesterday, Phillip said they both got in earlier.

They'd be here soon, I was sure of it. Until then, I'd keep poking away at the software, and pretending I had any idea what a realistic threesome would look like, lizard-enhanced gunman notwithstanding.

My phone chimed with a text from an unknown number.

We're in the big room. Come find us.

We? Where?

I locked my machine, grabbed my phone, and wandered toward the same room Dustin gave his presentation in yesterday. That was the only *big* room I could think of, but I still approached with hesitation.

As I drew closer, three familiar voices drifted out, one of them Luna, telling Dustin and Phillip what to do, using words like *router*, *CAT6*, and *hard-wired*. I rounded the corner to find the room transformed from yesterday, and the three of them at the center of the change.

A series of long tables filled the room, each with three computers behind, and three monitors, keyboards, and mice on top.

"Addie." Dustin grinned when he saw me. "Told you she'd understand."

"I really don't. The text was from you? What's going on?" On the surface, the *what* was obvious, but the *why* escaped me.

Luna pointed Dustin toward the last row of machines. "Finish checking the connectivity."

I wasn't used to seeing her bossy. It was cute. And a little terrifying.

"Everyone who wants to participate is doing the first beta in here today," Dustin said as he worked. "Partly because I thought it would be fun. Partly because Ms. Queen of Security said it was the best way to ensure no one hacked us while it happened."

Luna smirked and waggled her fingers in a

wave. "We're on an isolated network. We're hard-wired to everything, and we won't have voice chat."

"Wow. Are we really worried about that kind of breach?" I knew people were talking about this game, but with my limited understanding of what she was doing, this was some beyond-high-level setup.

"We're absolutely *not* worried, because we're doing things right." Luna climbed under one of the desks and fiddled with cables. "My job is to make sure people like me don't get in. I'd want in to this."

Luna was a talented, and potentially dangerous, hacker—it was why she was in charge of the company's digital security. In her case, the hacks tended to be for the challenge rather than the threat, but I understood her point. "So... what can I do?"

"Pick your faction." Phillip joined me, placing a hand at the small of my back.

A rush of heat flashed between us. "Can I be Erudite?"

"Not unless we want to get sued." Phillip planted me in front of a computer that was already on. "This one's good to go. We set it up for you. You can take the online quiz or just choose from the list of descriptions, it's up to you."

"Back up." I could guess at some of what he was saying, but that didn't mean it all fit together in a clear picture. "What and what and what?

Pretend I'm brand new here and start from the beginning."

Dustin took a deep breath. "In the beginning God created the heavens and the earth."

"Smart ass." I couldn't help laughing. "Today. What's going on in here and how am I involved?"

Phillip pulled up a chair next to mine. "We explained the beta. We wanted to bring the whole group together, like gaming parties used to be."

"I borrowed some competition equipment from Rinslet." Dustin sounded pleased with himself.

He should be. As far as I could tell, it was a nice setup.

"And the game has factions, based on who you are," Luna said. "They're not like guilds, and you can be in whatever one you pick, regardless of race or class, but they do come with bonuses and also wicked awesome crests. I wanted to tell you, but we've all been sworn to secrecy until the news goes out today."

"I'm starting to get the impression Dustin likes his secrets," I said.

He stared at me for a moment, expression blank. Did I insult him? His grin and wink were a relief. "I like a good, fun surprise. But this mandate didn't come from me."

Phillip reached past me to click through screens on my computer, and type. When he was leaned this close, the faint scent of musk and soap teased me. Great. He was gorgeous, intelligent, smelled good, and was well hung. That wasn't tempting at all.

Phillip pulled away, but not so much I no longer felt his heat. "We've all played the game in bits and pieces, but we're starting from the same place as everyone else for today's beta. We want to blend in with the other players and watch their experiences. Everyone else in the office already has their faction picked and their character built out, though. This is your chance to do the same before everything starts."

Dustin crawled out from the space he'd squeezed into behind a table holding a long, rectangular box with a lot of lights, and wires coming out of it. "Plus Phillip will add your faction symbol to your avatar for the forums."

"Oh yeah, I saw that yesterday." And with everything else, I completely forgot to ask what the playing card suits meant beneath everyone's pictures and why they didn't seem related to any of the teams or other groupings. "So which faction are each of you?"

Dustin, Phillip, and Luna exchanged looks.

"We'll tell you after you pick," Dustin said. "Everyone else went into this blind, you can too."

"Gee, thanks." I didn't mind, though. There was always time in life for another quiz that told me what color nail polish I would be or what kind of cheese toast I was. I loved those things. "Where's this digital sorting hat?"

Phillip winced. "You can't call it that."

"Picking panties?" I offered, then bit the inside of my cheek at how bad it sounded.

"Done." Dustin dropped into another chair and logged onto the computer in front of him.

Luna tapped him lightly on the shoulder. "What are you doing?"

"Drawing Picking Panties."

She shook her head. "You're testing network fidelity on router six, if you want all your players to stay connected for several hours."

"Yes, mistress." Dustin's sigh was exaggerated.

I couldn't help my laughter. This was definitely *not* the Luna I usually saw with my brother, but I could see how they were halves of the same person. "Picking Panty Quiz. Direct me."

Phillip reached past me again to click a bookmark in my web browser. Could he have just pointed it out? Sure. Was I glad he didn't? So very glad.

I clicked through the quiz, and impatiently waited the five-ish seconds for my results to load. I read from the screen. "Hearts. The god Lir is your patron, and your element is water. You're gifted with and drawn to the ways of cleansing and healing. Rebirth and resurrection are within your grasp, and you bring abundance to those you hold dear."

"I knew you'd be hearts," Luna said. "So perfect for you."

I wasn't sure I agreed, but I liked the hope in the description. "What are each of you?"

"I'm diamonds. My element is earth. It's abundance, but more in a *I know the hearts of men* kind of way." Luna recited the explanation as if she'd done it dozens of times before.

Dustin wiggled his fingers in wave. "Spades-slash-air. Words are my weapon of choice. Unless I need actual weapons, then those are awesome too."

"Clubs. Fire," Phillip said. "Single minded focus."

"And the four of us make up a perfect set." Luna clapped, glee on her face.

"Now, character creation." Dustin dropped into a chair on the other side of me.

"They're proud of this." Luna took a seat across the table from us, angled so I could see her next to the monitor. "They should be. It's the *coolest* character creation screen *ever*." This was the Luna I knew. Eyes bright, grin plastered on, and radiating infectious enthusiasm. "You can pick your race, character size, shape, male, female, neither, both, somewhere in between—"

"Hey, now." The reprimand in Dustin's voice sounded exaggerated. "You're stealing our thunder."

The exchange made me even more excited to

get into the setup and see what the whole thing was about. "I promise she's not. I need to know how you made everything scale and gave the designs the flexibility they needed to do what she's describing."

And they told me. For the next hour, the three of us geeked out on an artistically technical level that would put most people to sleep, but that I loved. *This* was what I signed on for. The reason I wanted to work for a company like this. It wasn't just making video game art, it was the innovation. The newness and uniqueness. The creativity and spark and being part of something vast.

"Last step, you get to pick your starting clothes. You can swap styles throughout the game, but you need to start somewhere," Dustin said.

I scrolled through the outfits and disappointment sank in. "Really?"

"What?" Dustin's hurt sounded real this time.

"I can either be super slutty or wear the dystopian version of a potato sack? You couldn't give me a Members Only jacket and stonewash jeans?"

Phillip sighed. "No. Because this is the 2080's, not the 1980's, and you are not that old."

"I'm mature for my age." Which was funnier when I was sixteen instead of thirty-seven.

I didn't necessarily have a problem with the outfits. They were gorgeously designed and detailed, and it was clear which bits were leather, cloth, and synthetic. But it was a little disappointing to see my Airmedic Nekokin—faith healer kitty-girl—dressed in an almost identical outfit to those I'd find in any other MMO—stomach bare, boobs barely covered, and ass not much better. "If I were playing the guy characters, what would my options be?"

"Exactly the same." Phillip scooted to the next computer over, woke it up, and flew his fingers across the keyboard. A moment later, a similar screen to mine appeared, but this one with a tall, slender character. He had alabaster skin, pointed ears, and wore a leather harness and briefs that looked more like thin strips of electrical tape crossed over his chest and crotch.

"Huh." I didn't expect that. It really was the same outfit my nekokin had access to. "Yay equality?"

Dustin sighed. "There are genre expectations. We had to stick to *some* rules."

"You think you could do better, I assume?" There was a challenge in Phillip's voice.

Could I? "I could do differently. *I'd* rather be wearing what I would design."

"You've done a lot of outfit design for games?" Dustin's tone wasn't condescending, but it did make me bristle.

As a matter of fact, I had. "We were raised in a strict, conservative household. My brother's version of *rebelling* was to mod video games to be what he wanted. He let me play, and he let me make clothes for the characters. Final Fantasy Seven was my favorite, and Tifa never looked more awesome."

"Sounds like she's volunteering." The fun was back in Dustin's voice.

Phillip nodded. "Adrienne's next task is to make *better* beginner outfits. And keep in mind, when we beta test, we're supposed to find things for *other* teams to fix."

Luna clapped. "Can we have wings?"

"Wings are for later in game," Phillip said as if it were obvious. "You have to earn the right to fly."

Luna stuck her tongue out at him. "Decorative wings. To hint at what's to come."

"Buy me coffee tomorrow morning, I'll give you wings." I wasn't above bribery when the cause was good.

Phillip sighed. "We retain veto power."

"Nope." Luna shook her head. "Adrienne says I get wings on my beginner clothes. I get wings."

Phillip, Dustin, and Luna gave me a brief tutorial on the controls, though it didn't take much. At least on the surface, the functionality was the same as most games out there. I was an odd blend of disappointed and relieved. Catching on fast would be easy, but I wanted the revolutionary game I'd been promised.

Dustin held out his little finger in a hook shape. "It's there. Pinkie swear."

"I didn't say anything." Which wasn't like me.

"Your expression said it all. And you're not the first to react this way." Dustin wiggled his finger. "Lincoln is top notch at intuitive user interface design."

"Damn right I am." A voice came from behind, and I realized people were joining us.

I hooked my pinkie through Dustin's. "Okay. Trusting you that the game gets more innovative as it goes on."

The groupings everyone sat in were similar to those I saw in the kick-off meeting. Dustin and Phillip took the spots on either side of me. Probably so we'd be in a team, but I liked being between them as a general idea.

Luna sat across from us, next to a woman with long, dark hair that cascaded in soft curls around her shoulders, and a slender man with dark hair and a sharp nose.

Dustin stood and whistled sharply. "I'll make this quick, because you all know why we're here. Dev is on speaker as well as wandering the room to take notes about any issues we find. You know how the game works. At least try to pretend we're as new as all the other players. Any questions? Good. Going live in ten. Nine. Eight."

I joined in the countdown with everyone else in the room, the collective excitement coursing through me. "Three. Two. One."

I half expected the servers to crash the instant we hit the top of the hour. But we were in the character lobby and then in the opening part of the game, a vast, neon cityscape spread out before us.

"Wow." I panned my camera around the landscape, and the reality of it all sank in. The men sitting next to me had built this visual. This entire look. The duo across from me, next to Luna, had given so many digital people stories. The guys on the phone had assembled all the pieces to make sure it flowed smoothly, it looked incredible...

It had never hit home before just what was required to build something like this, and my mind boggled as I absorbed it all. Dozens of other characters milled around mine. Aside from Phillip, I had no idea which were employees and which were beta testers.

"Come on, let's explore," Luna said.

Correction, I knew exactly who the blue-skinned, short, red headed elf was that stood across from my nekokin. Luna had picked the leather bandages outfit. The character snapped a metal hand, and a spark of blue flickered into sight before fading again.

"Sonya's going to show us something, come on." Luna's character motioned for mine to follow.

The large orc next to her waved, and Sonya said, "hello."

My avatar waved back, and I followed when

they took off. "Where are we going?" It was getting loud in here, with everyone shouting back and forth, and I loved it. Who needed voice chat when we could have a room full of excited gamers? The energy in the air was tangible and delicious.

"I want to play my favorite side quest," Sonya said.

"Strip club," Luna added.

Given the nature of the game and the promises made about content I couldn't help but wonder, "Won't the strip club be crowded?"

"Not this one. Not during beta." Sonya's soft voice barely carried over people shouting spells and directions and cheers.

When we arrived, I knew exactly why she'd said that. It was a male strip club with orcs. The lighting, textures, movement, and sound were all on point. It was incredible.

Sonya's orc led us to a table in the back of the room, where another orc sat, head in his hands. He wore a leather thong, a studded collar, and nothing else.

"He looks so good," Sonya said with awe.

"You described him perfectly." Phillip's reply was one of pride, and a glance showed his broad smile.

Luna nudged me under the table with her toes. "Talk to him."

I struck up a conversation with the orc, who

spun a sad tale of how his nekokin Dom was missing, and could we please help find him?

Of course I would. I clicked *Accept* and my game froze, flickered, and vanished, the desktop glaring back at me. I frowned and logged back in, only to have it happen again the instant I clicked *Accept* on the quest.

"Aww. This is one of my favorite early stories." Sonya pouted. "Hey, Chris, your code is broken," she hollered across the room.

Someone stepped up next to her. "Tell me everything that happened, step by step." Chris looked at me. "You're not supposed to break the game, noob." His tone was light, but a hint of irritation lay underneath it.

Luna's bristle matched mine.

"That's exactly what she's supposed to do, twink." Dustin leaned in, arm pressing against mine.

Twink could mean a lot of things. I assumed in this case it was a counter to *noob*. As in, a long-time player who creates a lower level character and gears them up to the max specifically to stomp on newbies.

Chris's smile didn't reach his eyes. "I'm giving her shit. Come on, we're all family here."

"Dude," Elliot, the developer from the meeting yesterday, called. "I'll take their feedback. Keep circling."

Chris rolled his eyes and walked away.

Elliot spent the next ten or fifteen minutes asking us for step-by-step details about what we'd been doing, asking Sonya and Luna to mimic the steps I'd taken, and doing a lot of tapping on his screen.

With our current plan crashed, Luna, Sonya, and I agreed to a warehouse raid with Phillip, Dustin, and Brandon.

I was the healer. And Sonya with her heavy armor and defense skills, plus Dustin with speed, damage, and medium armor, promised to protect me. Phillip wielded a bio magic, similar to Luna's, and Brandon got up close and personal with the baddies, fighting with his fists, and occasionally offering me healing backup, though his magic wasn't as powerful as mine.

It was clear we all knew our classes, but we weren't used to each other's fighting patterns or rhythms. We got our asses kicked, but we pulled out a victory, with Phillip and me as the last characters standing.

It was a blast. I loved being surrounded by this feeling of excitement and an obvious passion for this creation of theirs.

When the pizza showed up around one, I was surprised so much time had passed. Later, when the game timer counted off the final thirty minutes, I was bummed to see it all coming to an end for the day.

The beta server went offline. Silence sank into the room, like the world was holding its breath, and then Dustin shouted, "That, was *fucking epic.*"

Cheers and yells of excitement erupted around me. I found myself on the receiving end of high fives from as many people as everyone else, and hugs from Luna, Sonya, and Phillip.

This was incredible. I had no idea what I'd done to land myself in the middle of such an amazing place, but I was so giddy to be a part of it.

7 /
dustin

Three days of beta. Three days of seeing the world play the game we'd built. Three days of *epicness*.

I grinned like an idiot the entire time we were loading loaner computers back into my SUV. Phillip and Adrienne were cleaning up the conference room, while Brandon and Jeremy helped me fit everything in my vehicle.

The early reviews were fantastic—of course—but Brandon and Jeremy had opted not to read them. Brandon already knew people were going to love the music, and Jeremy said he didn't read reviews. Any of them. Apparently he'd managed to avoid them most of his career.

It was a writer thing, he told me.

"That's the last of it." Brandon tossed a bundle of cables into a crate in the front seat. "Tonight?"

"Looking forward to it." Watching Danny and

Reese on stage was always fun, and it would be the perfect end to a perfect week.

"Dustin, a minute?" Judith joined us behind the building.

Never tell the boss *no*, especially when I was working to convince her I wanted that Director job. "Sure."

"We'll catch you later." Brandon waved, and he and Jeremy headed back inside.

She waited until they were gone, before speaking again. "I sent the information to Legal that you gave me. It looks good, thanks."

"Any time." I knew where the balance lay between a casual tone and a professional one and I summoned it now. "I'm sorry this came down on us."

"Not your fault. As long as the asshole backs off, it doesn't matter. I'm hearing a lot of good things about the beta this week, both internally and from fans and streamers."

I couldn't help my grin. "Because this game is going to blow them out of the water. Everyone I've talked to loved the company-sanctioned gaming we did in the conference room. Thank you for permission to set that up." I wasn't above reminding her of the awesome things I'd done. Every conversation was a chance to push how good I'd be if she promoted me.

"Keep it up," Judith said. "I want to see more of this kind of teamwork."

"You don't even have to ask."

"Go. Return this crap. Tell them I send my thanks." She patted the back of my SUV, where the computer equipment sat.

I gave her a salute. "Yes, ma'am."

She rolled her eyes and walked back into the building.

I did one last mental check, making sure everything I'd borrowed was going back, and I headed to Rinslet.

Was this part of my job? The hype? The build-up both internally and externally?

No.

Was I going to keep doing it anyway?

Damn right.

I'd flitted through a lot of jobs in my life, thanks to a knack for picking up new things and running with them. The art had been at my core for as long as I could remember, but it wasn't my *job* until Rinslet. Like Adrienne, like so many of the people at Rinslet, I was hired for my talent rather than experience, and given a chance to step into a highly sought after job.

Unlike Phillip, Brandon, and most of the others at Aces, I was older when I was hired. I'd been doing the video game art for less than a decade, and some of my colleagues were going on twenty years. No one worked for the same company for twenty years in tech. Especially in the cutting-edge jobs. While it was true, Aces was a new company, they were really Rinslet 2.0. Aside from Adrienne and Luna, I was the *new guy*.

At Rinslet I'd found a group of people I wanted to work with, but it was still just a job.

When we all started talking about this game, when Judith said she could fund it, I was all in. This was a project I was fully behind, not specifically because of the extra options for characters to fuck, but it was new. It was groundbreaking. The game itself was brilliant. I wanted the world to love it as much as I did.

Maybe *the world* was asking for a bit much, but I was willing to push every limit to get our name out there. Aces didn't have a marketing or client-facing group specifically—it wasn't in our budget. Since everyone at Rinslet had media training, we'd decided we could handle spreading the word in other ways.

And I was God damn fucking determined to make that happen.

I'd hate to take the Director position from Phillip, who had become my closest friend over the past few years, but he'd been up front about not wanting a management job if it only involved bossing people around. He wanted to mentor.

Maybe it hadn't made sense to put me in charge

of a two person team, but Brandon was the only one in Music, and he had a director spot, while an office sat empty in the Art room, waiting for my name to be on it.

I pulled into the loading docks at Rinslet, and Chloe was waiting for me with a couple of younger guys I didn't recognize. This company came from humble beginnings, just like Aces, and now they had their own eight story building in the middle of downtown, with their name in big bold letters on the glass.

We were going to hit this point, and it was going to happen long before I retired.

After I parked, I greeted her with a smile and a wave, opened the back of the truck, and grabbed a box of keyboards.

"Let them do the work." Chloe jerked her thumb at the guys. "I wanna talk game." She was a few years younger than me, probably about Adrienne's age, but I wanted to be Chloe when I grew up. She'd started in writing when she was fresh out of high school, had created the core storyline for Rinslet's most popular game, and now ran a large portion of the company.

I stepped aside and let her minions grab their first load of equipment. When they had disappeared inside, I asked, "What do you think?"

Her eyes grew wide with what I assumed was supposed to look like innocence. "I'm not

73

supposed to have access to your beta. I'm the competition."

"Uh-huh." I chuckled. "Should I ask who gave you a key, or are we going to play the *I heard from a friend of a friend?*" It was probably Judith who let her into the beta. Or Scott. He was a half owner of Rinslet, and a silent investor in Aces. He kept the latter quiet mostly to let us rise on our own merits, and not at all because he didn't want his name associated with our game.

Chloe shrugged and her smile never faded. "Let's just say Santa visited early, but my feedback is firsthand. Are you following the early reviews?"

"Duh." The bad was exactly what I expected—people hated it either for the smut content or the diversity, and frequently both. But the good was *really* good. "But what did *you* think?"

"It's incredible. Seriously. It's visually stunning, the fight mechanics are spot-on, and Sonya and Jeremy did a bang-up job with the side quests. We get to see the main story soon, right?"

"I can't tell you that."

She raised her eyebrows. Yeah, we both knew I was full of it. She wasn't going to tell anyone.

"As long as bug fixes go well this round and next, we're opening up the first twenty levels in two weeks. Main story and all."

Chloe grinned. "I have a *huge* favor to ask. Feel free to tell me *no*, but I will beg if it'll help."

"As long as it won't get me fired, or arrested or killed I guess, ask away."

"*Santa* only brought me one beta key. I don't suppose next round I could get a second one for Jordan."

Jordan was Chloe's boyfriend, and someone else I had mad respect for. I'd been hired to replace Jordan when he was fired over a bullshit public scandal, so we'd never worked together, but the guy was wicked talented and a blast at parties. "Only because it's you and him," I said.

Her grin spread. "You're the best. Seriously. I owe you."

"I'm not keeping score, but if I were, right now we're more than even." I jerked my thumb at the computer equipment she'd helped me secure. "Tell him to check his email in a couple of days."

We chatted a little longer as we helped her guys finish unloading the SUV, mostly gossip about who'd been promoted and who had moved on to other things, and I was on my way.

Man it had been a great week. The beta. Addie.

Whispers of her perfume, or whatever it was, teased my memories. I may not be able to describe a scent, but I knew exactly how she looked, and the woman did amazing things to a lightweight camisole with a button-down open over it.

She should join us tonight at the club. To celebrate. She was part of the team, after all. And she was probably even more fun outside the office than in. She had that quiet *girl next door* attractiveness, with just the right blend of life experience and naïveté. I didn't know quite how she made that work, but *fuck* I liked it.

I dialed her at the next stop light and put her on speaker.

"Hello?" Her voice was sweet and hesitant. I bet she was insatiable behind closed doors.

Or wanted to be. "Hey, it's Dustin. What are you doing tonight?"

"Not a clue. Nachos and bad sci-fi movies? Am I being graded on my answer?"

I laughed. "Nope. No grades. A couple of us are going to celebrate an awesome week and head to a local club. You should meet us there."

"What kind of club?" Like that, the hesitation was back.

"The kind with beer and live music. Brandon's boyfriend Danny is performing."

"Oh. Okay. Sure." And now she was light again.

What? "What other kinds of clubs are there?" I had a list in my head, but I needed to know what she was thinking.

"The kind with collars and leather and whips and... you know. A girl hears stories about orgies, and starts to wonder— Never mind."

Was she the kind of woman who wanted to be cuffed and collared? Maybe. But something told me

Addie was more a strip-me-down-in-front-of-an-audience-and-make-me-come-while-they-watch kind of gal.

Like that, I was hard. Did a series of celebrations filled with everyone screwing everyone sound like fun? Yeah, but mostly to the part of me that was still twenty. I wasn't up for weekend orgies these days. Drawing the extra limbs was hard enough. Keeping track of them during actual sex? No thanks.

Whoever I was dating tended to be plenty when I wanted to get laid, and when I didn't have that option, Phillip was always a great fuck. But I might consider a threesome if Addie was involved.

"Nope, just the normal kind of loud, obnoxious, fun bar-type club," I said.

"Sounds great. When and where?"

Yes. How was I so excited about such a simple answer? "Eight, so you've got time. I'll text you the info when I get home."

I might need to do something else when I got home, like take a little life advice from *Something About Mary*. Get rid of the raging hard-on digging into my jeans, so I could focus on the evening out.

8 /
adrienne

I t was a night at a bar with co-workers. So why was I going through my closet, my pulse hammering in my ears, as I looked for the perfect outfit like I was getting ready for a hot date?

Because my co-workers were sizzling. I knew exactly who it was when Dustin called, I just didn't know why he was calling me. When he texted me on the first day of beta testing, I'd saved his number. Re-read the silly note several times. And I'd been fixated on any praise from Phillip the same way. Every piece of encouragement he'd given me this week about my art was etched in my mind.

It was possible I had fantasies of doing anything he asked, as long as it was followed by *good girl*.

I needed to rein those thoughts in now. The two had been understanding about the random, weird things I tended to blurt out, but my word vomit would get a lot worse if I was daydreaming about fucking them while I was with them at the club.

Tonight was a night out with friends, and I wasn't going to look like I was trying too hard. I'd pushed away a lot of my friends during my marriage to Sean, and I missed both them and just hanging out.

I moved aside little black dresses, a leather skirt, and a lace top that would be completely see-through without something underneath, to grab a faded Foo Fighters concert Tee to go with my favorite pair of jeans.

Heavy eyeliner and bright red lipstick finished the look. I stared at myself in the mirror for several seconds. Too much? Not enough?

If I was with friends, I'd do this. It was perfect.

The club wasn't downtown. It was at the edge of a shopping center in Sugar House. The sign out front boasted live bands almost every night, and the parking lot was only about half full.

At least it should be easy to find the guys. I stepped inside, pausing just out of the flow of traffic to scan the room. The lights were low, but it was still easy to see that the tables weren't any more full than the lot had been. Photos of bands lined the walls, several of them taken in this room.

"*Addie.*" Dustin's shout carried about the loud chatter and drew my gaze and a smile. He waved me over to a table where Phillip and Brandon also sat, near the stage. Not that far from the stage was a huge difference. "What are you drinking?" He asked when I reached them.

"Cranberry juice."

"With Vodka?"

"No... Just cranberry juice." Because I was ninety, apparently. Also because I'd skipped dinner in the process of pretending I wasn't obsessing about tonight, and I had to drive myself home.

"Don't mind him," Brandon said. "He doesn't know how to react to people not drinking on his dime."

Phillip pulled out the empty chair next to him and gestured for me to sit. "Not his fault. *Free booze* is the mating call of most sales representatives."

"You make it sound like I'm fucking them." Dustin set a glass of juice in front of me.

How did he do that? I hadn't seen him leave or order.

"Nope. Pretty sure they're the ones doing the fucking." Brandon clucked.

I'd only talked to Brandon a few times in the last couple of days, but I liked him. One thing surprised me, though. "You said celebration, I figured more of the office would be here."

"Most of the people we work with aren't really..." The way Phillip wrinkled his nose was more like thought than distaste, "...bar people."

I understood that. Graham and Cole weren't

either. I would've asked about inviting Luna, when Dustin called, but Cole had taken all three of them off the grid for the weekend. It was the only way he could guarantee Luna and Graham would put away the tech.

"Their loss." Brandon twisted his seat toward the stage. "You'll never hear a better band than this."

Looking at the fact that every other table in the room was empty, I had my doubts. Brandon was probably biased. I didn't need *the best*, though. I was here for the atmosphere, the company, and the view.

On the stage, a man with tattoos covering both arms and climbing up his neck from his tank top, stepped up to the mic. "All right, gang. We've got a favorite back tonight. Let's show Plaid Peanut Butter how much we love them."

The loud whistles and hollers that came from our table, drowning out the lack of the same anywhere else in the room, were reminiscent of Dustin's *rally* earlier this week.

I liked being part of the group here to have fun.

A drumbeat played over the bar sound system, simple at first, but growing in complexity.

Brandon leaned toward me. "That's Reese. She can't sing and drum at the same time, so she pre-records."

I barely knew more than the average person about music, and only because my parents were convinced that learning to play flute would be good for me, but I liked what I was hearing.

A heavy guitar riff joined the beat, and a blond man with an easy smile and hair buzzed close to his scalp stepped onto stage, his fingers flying wicked fast up and down the neck of his guitar. I recognized Danny from the photos Brandon kept in his office, but a still shot didn't capture the energy he radiated.

The lights flickered and blinked out, but the music never stopped.

"Wait for it." Phillip's whisper blended with, and helped build, the anticipation.

A glow started from the lights around the stage, growing and expanding through the room, and illuminating a woman center stage with a wireless mic in hand.

Pin-straight violet hair hung around her shoulders and halfway down her back, framing an elf-like face decorated with triangle sunglasses. Her collar had spikes and her vinyl jacket hugged her tightly enough her breasts looked like they might pop out if she bent in a certain way. The way her hair flew and caught the light with each bob of her head said it was a wig.

But when she opened her mouth and the opening line to *Amen* by Halestorm came out, nothing mattered except her voice and the backup music and vocals.

I was captivated. The next hour passed in a wave of incredible music—some covers, some original music—that grabbed me by the soul and held me tight.

When Reese announced they were going to take a break, I felt like I could breathe again, and at the same time was disappointed at the pause in the experience.

"Well?" Brandon watched me expectantly.

"Holy shit, wow," was the best I could manage.

Brandon grinned. "Told you so."

"How... That is..." There was no way *I* was at a loss for words. "How do more people not know about them? Where is everyone? Why aren't you running their hype machine?" I asked Dustin.

Dustin winced, and Brandon's smile faltered. "It's complicated," Brandon said. "Short version is, shitty contract."

"Ouch."

Brandon nodded. "Pretty much. What do you think of your first week here?"

I still wanted to screw the men I shared an office with, or watch them screw, or do anything with them that involved nakedness. Oh, and the art and tech were amazing. It took a lot of restraint to keep all of that from popping out of my mouth. "It's everything I was promised, and more. Especially the nakedness." *Damn it.*

"If you've heard any of Cole's stories, you probably expected that," Brandon said.

I shook my head. "Does Cole really strike you as a *story* person? Besides, I'd rather not ask for details about that part of his life." I held up my hands. "Don't misunderstand, I don't have a problem with listening to stories about all of you fucking—" I winced. I could gloss over that. "—but talking about my brother's boyfriend's sex life is a step away from talking about my brother's sex life, and I'm going to draw a line before we take that step."

Brandon laughed. "That's fair."

"You may need to get used to it," Phillip said. "We'll respect your wishes, but this entire industry is incestuous."

Dustin wrinkled his nose. "Really? You couldn't use a better word?"

Brandon shrugged. "I mean, Cole is Judith's ex, and Judith stole us from Step Daddy Scott and Zach."

"Ugh, could you not call them that?" The new voice drew my attention to Danny and Reese, who had joined us. Danny settled into Brandon's lap without hesitation.

That was sweet.

"They're sexy," Reese said. "How many tech execs can say that, *and* keep it up for two decades."

"Too. Much. Alpha." Danny draped an arm around Brandon's neck.

Reese rolled her eyes. "I want a lap." She looked at Dustin.

Envy pinged my thoughts. What would it be like to be so bold and just claim a spot on some smart, sexy guy's lap? Specifically, *Dustin's* lap.

I felt a twinge better when Dustin shook his head. "Mine's not open."

"Most boring party boy ever." Reese's grumble didn't hold any malice.

And Dustin didn't look bothered. "Seriously, convince a few other people of that, and *I'll* sit on *your* lap."

And there was the jealousy again.

"I feel like you're missing the point," Reese said.

"You're the one without a lap. Sounds like you're missing the point," Phillip countered.

Brandon punched him lightly in the arm. "Dude, inappropriate."

"Fuck you." Phillip's tone was light.

"Can I watch?" Danny asked with an enthusiasm I understood intensely, given the implication.

Reese cleared her throat. "Are you volunteering?" She stared at Phillip.

He raised an eyebrow and kept his mouth shut.

Reese huffed, looked between the men, and nudged me upright. Next thing I knew, I had a lap full of Reese. "You're not my last choice, cross my heart," she said. "But we're strangers, and I don't want to scare you off your first night here."

"I'm fine with that." I wasn't sure with what. Her taking a seat. And that it wasn't on Dustin or Phillip. Was I being possessive? Apparently.

"I'm Reese, by the way. That's Danny, in case you haven't been told. You probably prefer to be called something other than *New Girl*."

"Adrienne."

She managed to shake my hand without displacing herself. "Pleasure to meet me." She grinned. "You loved the show." It wasn't a question, and she wasn't wrong.

"You were amazing. Both of you, but, *you*. You're like Shirley Manson, in person. And younger. And prettier." I could shut up now, please. "You seriously wail."

"Blasphemy." Danny sounded horrified.

Reese stared at him.

He grinned. "I didn't say I disagreed." He extracted himself from Brandon's lap, and the two shared a long kiss. "Gotta get back for the second act."

Reese stood as well. "Great meeting you, Adrienne New Girl. Next song is for you."

"What does that mean?" I asked as Reese and Danny walked back toward the stage.

"I assume it's a pre-emptive dedication," Brandon said. "Beyond that... I never try to guess with Reese."

The music started again, and Danny plucked out the familiar notes of *Bad Romance* by Lady Gaga. While I loved the song, why did Reese think it was appropriate for me? It couldn't be the relationship I just got out of. Was it for some future she assumed awaited me? Was I reading *way* too much into the entire thing?

Most likely.

We stayed for the rest of the show, and it was after eleven when things finally wound down. It would be a while before I did, though. The vibe in this place, at our table, had me buzzing with the kind of giddiness I hadn't been able to lose myself in for a while.

I didn't have an excuse to linger here, as much as I wanted one. "I should get going." I reluctantly pushed myself away from the table, and forced myself to stand.

"We'll walk you out. Make sure you get to your car safely," Dustin said.

"You guys good?" Phillip asked Brandon.

"We've got it. See you all Monday."

I asked him to tell Reese and Danny again that they were amazing, then headed outside with Dustin and Phillip.

"You really loved it," Dustin said.

Was it that obvious? "It was so much fun." Excitement hummed in my veins, and the cool kiss of the night air brushed my heated cheeks. "I know it's only been four days, but this job is like the best thing ever."

Dustin looked skeptical. "The best? I mean, we're awesome, but that's a high bar."

"Better than sex?" Phillip asked.

A short laugh escaped before I could stop it. "In my life? Going to the grocery store is better than sex." No. Stop. Don't do this, Adrienne. "Why do you think I have such a hard time drawing it?" *Fuck.* Apparently I was doing this.

Dustin *tsked*. "That's not right."

"It's really not. There should be a law or something that a woman my age should already know—" I snapped my jaw shut.

"Know what?" Phillip asked.

What gets me off besides a bullet vibrator and free porn. At least I still had some restraint. "What falls between unfulfilling vanilla fucking and paid actors doing it for the camera." But not much.

"I can show you that." Phillip's confidence and lack of hesitation made my stomach drop into my shoes.

"Dude—"

Phillip held up a finger, silencing Dustin, and looked at me, as we stopped by my car. "You do the nude sketching already. And the other night wasn't your first time in that classroom." The intensity in his gaze seared into me.

"Yes. And no, it wasn't my first time. I like

learning about the lines in anatomy."

"You've got a solid foundation," Phillip said. "I'm not talking about anything inappropriate." He glanced at Dustin. "Clothes on, and just a few pointers about what falls in that middle ground, for work."

I couldn't think of an argument. I didn't want to. Should I be worried about work? If I asked, would the offer be withdrawn? He said clothes on. It wasn't like we were actually going to screw. "I'm not going to get the right perspective if I'm in the middle of it."

"I've got a camera set up at home. We'll capture it, you'll have reference shots for later," Dustin said.

Anticipation and desire surged inside, lighting my senses up and pulsing between my legs. Did he just offer to film me in naughty positions? A teeny tiny prick of logic said that was a bad idea, but it was one of the hottest suggestions I'd ever heard. "Okay. I'm in."

"Perfect." Phillip's immediate reply made it easier for me to not take back my agreement.

I should say *never mind. Forget it.* "When?"

"We're free right now." Phillip opened my car door for me. "Dustin will text you the address. Meet us there?"

I nodded, not sure what I was more terrified of hearing come out of my mouth—a take back or a gushing acceptance.

9 /
phillip

First time I saw this room in Dustin's house, one question popped into my head before any others.

"Did you used to be... a cam boy?" There was Adrienne, mimicking my thoughts. "I thought..."

That we weren't making porn.

Dustin's chuckle was kind. "I wasn't and we're not." He flicked on the row of overhead lights meant for more neutral lighting, rather than the dimmer, more seductive mood the other bank offered. "I've done a lot of jobs in my life, and this was one of them."

He gestured at a room that looked straight out of a catalog page—queen sized bed with matching, soft colored bedding and a headboard stained the same way as the dresser and vanity table.

Yup, straight out of a catalogue photo shoot,

including the tripods, and cameras locked away on the opposite side of the room.

"And by *this* you don't mean porn." Adrienne was skeptical.

I had to clear the air. "Boudoir shoots."

"Ahh." Understanding spread over her face.

Dustin made his way to the cabinet with the electronics, pulled out a video recorder, and attached it to one of the tripods. "Turns out a lot of men get the wrong idea when someone like me photographs their significant other in sexy lingerie. Or less."

"So, um, what do we do now?" Adrienne must have suddenly found her shoes fascinating. The abrupt shyness made her sexier.

"Dustin, what kind of room do we have to maneuver?" I asked. He and I had used the room a few times for a range of projects, but they'd all been still shots. I'd specifically promised Adrienne *clothes on* because the thought of teasing her, stripping her down, and fucking her until she screamed with ecstasy, all in front of a camera, gave me a full-on chubby.

And if she was as timid and inexperienced with sex as she claimed, I wasn't the guy to help her discover whether or not she was capable of no-strings-fucking.

Dustin pointed at the floor. "Keep it on the rug, including the bed, and the camera will catch it."

Smart man.

I loosely grasped Adrienne's hand and led her to the approximate middle of the rug. "Where do you want to start?"

She shrugged, but didn't pull her hand away, despite not meeting my gaze. "Pretend I don't know anything about anything." Her head flew up. "I do. Know some things. Not nearly as many as I probably should at my age, but I was married, I'm not a virgin, I'm just not—" She clenched her jaw shut.

God, how desperately I wanted to help her figure out what she really liked. And possibly beat the shit out of an ex-husband who hadn't done that with her. Nah, I wasn't a violent guy. I'd just make sure he knew what he'd missed out on.

"We'll start at the beginning, and work our way up." I stepped behind her and angled us to face Dustin. "Stop me if you need to, for any reason."

"I'm sure it'll be fine." Her reply was quiet.

I wasn't so certain, but it was time to embrace my inner teenager and figure out how much we could get up to without ever leaving first base. I pressed into Adrienne's back and slid my hands along her hips, to link my fingers and rest my palms on her stomach.

Her quiet sigh was fuel spilling through my veins.

"I'm not *that* inexperienced," she said.

I leaned my head in, mouth near her ear. She

smelled like strawberries and Reese's perfume. "You said the beginning."

"I did. Please, keep going."

And now I wanted to hear her actually begging. Instead, I glided my hands higher, over her shirt, to lightly cup her breasts.

At her gasp, I was rock hard, my erection pressing into the soft curve of her ass.

"We expect this will be one of our more popular emotes." I managed to keep my voice even and resist the desire to knead gently. "We'll need variations on it in the future, so feel free to think about what you'd like to see done differently."

"Sounds hard." She paused, then shook her head with a laughing-sigh. "You know what I mean."

I very distinctly knew what she meant. "Next up…" I glided a hand down her stomach, over her jeans, to cover her crotch. Her hips bucked toward my touch, and it took all of my restraint to keep from responding. "Visually there's not much to that one, but it's a favorite of mine."

"Same. We have so much in common."

I smiled and spun her to face me, turning us both at the same time so our sides were to the camera. I ran a hand along her ass, down the back of her leg, and hooked her knee to pull it up to my hip. "You see a lot of this in porn." My hips itched to press closer. "And this is the kind of thing we're avoiding in game."

Her giggle was breathy and pink flushed her face and neck. "If that's the case, why show me?"

"So you can see how completely impractical it is in real life. Can you imagine trying to fuck like this?"

"Believe me, I'm trying."

Me too. "But no?"

She shook her head. "Maybe... No. Not even if I were fifteen years younger."

"This, on the other hand." I let go of her leg to draw a light touch along her jaw and over her neck, before knotting my fingers in her hair with a soft yank.

She whimpered, and I instinctively tightened my grip. I tugged harder, coaxing her to her knees. The way she looked up at me, eyes wide and hungry, was a mirror to my soul.

Her smirk came out of nowhere. "Big surprise. I'm familiar with blow jobs."

Of course she was. Selfish, inconsiderate ex. "How about this then?" I helped her to her feet, and pressed my body to hers as I angled her toward the bed. "Lie on your back."

She did.

I didn't give Adrienne time to consider if this was awkward, as I moved in to prop one of her legs up. I knelt between her thighs. Despite this all being a mime act, I couldn't help but apply enough pressure to make sure she felt it, as I ran my fingertips up the inside of her thighs, and pressed higher, in every spot I wanted my mouth to be. My head followed the path, diving between her legs.

Having my face this close to her pussy and not being able to take a taste was cruel and unusual punishment, I was pretty sure. Especially when her heavy breathing mingled with the hammering of my pulse in my ears.

"What else?" I asked as I pulled away and tugged her into a sitting position. We hadn't covered much, but realistically, the average person only screwed in so many positions. As I adjusted myself, both my seat and my dick, I caught a glimpse of Dustin, who watched us, not the camera, with open lust and desire.

"How does it work with more than two people? *Actually* work?" Adrienne's question drew my attention again. Her lips were bright, despite her lipstick having faded hours ago, and she alternated between biting and licking the bottom one.

I wanted to lean in and do that for her. "Dustin, leave the camera running, and join us." I lay down next to Adrienne, and patted my legs. "Straddle me."

She did, resting her ass a few inches above my knees.

"*No one's* dick is that long," I teased. "In real life or in game. Scoot up."

Adrienne ducked her head, and didn't budge.

I rested my hands on her knees, teasing my thumbs along the inside of her legs, and urged her closer. Her weight and heat pressed through two layers of denim to tease my cock.

"Like this?" Her question was breathless.

"Perfect." More of a growl slid into my reply than I intended. I swallowed hard and summoned the last threads of my composure, to sound normal. "The trick is making room for multiple bodies, in a way that at least tries to prevent leg cramps."

Dustin knelt behind Adrienne.

I trailed my hands up her ass and over her back, pulling her chest to mine, and Dustin moved to press in behind her.

"And sex is possible like this?" Each breath Adrienne took shuddered through me.

"Possible. Fun. It just takes a little coordination and timing." I returned my hands to her hips to grip tight, and rocked her in short strokes, while I thrust with my hips. Strictly to prove my point.

Then Adrienne was grinding against me on her own. Her eyelids fluttered while she licked her lips and dry humped me.

I was captivated. And probably about thirty seconds from coming in my jeans, like I was a kid again. It would be worth it. I drew a thumb along her bottom lip.

She gasped and her eyes flew wide open. "So those are the basics, right?" She rolled off me and far enough away to break all contact with both Dustin and me.

That sucked. But it was a good indicator that I was right to not push for more. "Those are the basics."

"It's later than I thought, I should go." Adrienne scurried to her feet. "Thank you for the help. You'll send me a link to the file on the cloud or something?" she asked Dustin. "For reference, of course."

"Yeah. Of course." Dustin's voice was thick with lust.

She took a few steps toward the door. "I should get going."

"Once you've reviewed, let us know what else you need to see." I couldn't have the night end on an off note. We all had to look each other in the eye on Monday.

Adrienne's smile flickered through her discomfort. "I will. Thank you for a great night. All of it."

"I'll walk you out." I had to adjust myself again when I stood. It was tempting to stay here. Fuck Dustin. Cuddle after? Nope. I didn't know where that impulse came from, but I wasn't indulging it.

"I'll call you in the morning, Phillip," Dustin called as we left.

Adrienne and I were quiet as we headed outside. But her smile and *thank you* were genuine when we reached her car. I waited until she was on the road, then headed out as well. The instant I got home, I was going to beat off until I was raw.

10 /
adrienne

What just happened to me?

I knew. The images were vivid in my mind as I drove home. The sensations of Phillip touching *everywhere*. Of Dustin pressing into my back.

I'd never been so turned on. I desperately wanted more, but at the same time, what little we did almost made me explode. When Phillip pushed me to my knees, I wanted to drag his zipper down with my teeth and taste him. Did people really do that? I couldn't stop thinking about him between my legs, his tongue gliding up my slit while Dustin watched. While some anonymous person on the other side of the camera watched, and Dustin joined us.

My hand drifted between my legs again, toward the throb that wouldn't stop. I so badly wanted relief.

As I navigated on mostly auto-pilot, I turned the corner near a small park. It was barely a single playground, and the lights in the back corner of the parking lot were out.

Need and inspiration overrode anything else, and I parked my car in the darkness. It was almost two in the morning, and there was no one around.

Would I care if there was?

I shut off the car. The sudden still drove home how empty but open this space was. Anybody could walk by.

I pushed my jeans and panties down to the crease where my legs met my hips, and glided my fingers between my thighs. I was so wet. Every moment from Dustin's room played out in my head, but more vividly. Our clothes came off.

What if one of them caught me now, fingering myself in a parking lot? They'd better offer to help.

I didn't need any teasing or build-up. I stroked my swollen clit hard to the wash of memories and fantasy. Orgasm sped up hard and fast, washing over me, but I didn't want to stop. I still needed more.

I rubbed until my hand and core ached, before I finally pulled away. I sucked my fingers clean, one at a time. That was new for me, but right now the taste was as much a turn on as everything else.

It took me a while to catch my breath and

regain my senses. When I did, I cleaned myself up with napkins from the glove compartment, and finished my drive home.

The memory of tonight was going in the *use over and over* bin for sure.

I woke up to streams of mid-morning sunlight warming my face, through blinds I'd forgotten to close last night.

Last night. The memories and heat flooded back on a fluffy cloud of lust. Did I really do that in the park? Did we really all do that before?

If I hadn't bolted, would Phillip have kissed me? Would we have moved past the *clothes on* stage? Would I have been able to look them in the eye on Monday morning? It really felt like the two of them had experience with the *no emotional attachment* part of a relationship. Could I ever do something like that?

The question bounced in my head while I stripped out of the rest of my clothes and climbed into the shower.

I hadn't been able to draw that line with Sean, but I'd learned so much since then. About people. About myself. I certainly didn't trust myself in a relationship. Not now. Maybe not ever again.

Okay, so that was a bit melodramatic, but it would be a while. I still had so much to learn about me. Moments like last night seemed like one of those things I wanted to add to that *who am I* list. How did someone even go about finding casual hookups?

Probably not by asking the guys I worked with. Though, the desire to be with them again, but more intimately was intense, and the desire to hook up with anyone long term was non-existent.

I finished my shower, toweled off, and ran a comb through my hair, leaving it in loose, damp strands around my shoulders. I wasn't seeing anyone today, so I might as well be comfortable in my favorite faded shorts, and oversized T-shirt.

Did Dustin send me that footage yet? I scrolled through my phone, to see if the email was there.

My doorbell rang. Must be a wrong house. Or missionaries. When I yanked the door open, and saw Sean on the other side, I cursed building management again for not putting peepholes in the doors.

"Adrienne. I'm glad I caught you." His smile wasn't warm or friendly, and he stepped into my apartment without waiting for permission.

What was he doing here? He wasn't supposed to have this address. A knot of fear formed in my gut, and I tried to reconcile it. Sean had never hurt me physically, but before a week ago, I also wouldn't have guessed he was the guy who would track me down, again and again, to get my attention.

"Actually, I'm just about to head out. I'm waiting for a call now." I held up my phone, and pressed the *phone* button and the first number on the *recents* list while I wiggled it. "Oh, there it is now."

I put the device to my ear, not caring that it was still ringing. "Hey." I hoped my greeting sounded normal. Could I fake a conversation with no one? Who had I called and what would they do if they picked up? "Yeah, I can go now."

"Hey, Addie." Dustin's voice rang in my ear when he answered.

He'd either play along or he wouldn't. How hard could it be? People did this on TV all the time. "That's fine. No worries. My place or yours?"

"What are you—"

"Yeah, totally." I cut Dustin off, and tried to ignore Sean's scrutiny. "If you come here, you can see Sean again."

"Is he there now?" Dustin's tone shifted from confusion to something deeper.

There was no way this would work. Sean would find out and he'd be pissed and then things would be worse. "Ten minutes sounds great. I mean, I'm ready now, so whatever."

"We're on our way," Dustin said.

I faked a smile and hoped it looked real. "Love you too. See you soon." I disconnected, my heart hammering against my ribs. "They'll be here soon," I said to Sean. "Let's schedule something."

"Who was that?" He didn't move.

"Dustin. My *boyfriend* you met the other day? Who else would I say *love you* to?"

"You used to say it to me. I don't know how many other men you're stringing along."

My anger cranked to match my nervousness. "I'm not *stringing along* anyone. Are you going to stick around to see him? He *really* wants to see you." Could I intimidate Sean into leaving? Dustin said he was on his way, but I didn't know what that meant.

"Cool. I'd love a chance to talk to him again." Sean crossed his arms and leaned against a nearby wall. "I can't believe you're dating an asshole like that."

"You don't even know him." Neither did I, but nothing about him set off warning bells. Then again, neither had Sean at first.

Sean sneered. "Guys like that are two-dimensional and straight out of a bad movie. He's probably a gym rat who would rather bench press than spend time with his woman, and he only goes out with you because you're plain and easy. I actually care about you."

I clenched my fists, biting back the sudden surge of tears and hurt. *This* was the Sean I knew, and I wouldn't let him tear me down. "That's not true." Great comeback, Adrienne. I jammed my hands in my pockets to keep them from shaking my whole body apart. "You should go."

"I want to talk, and we can do that before he gets here."

"About what?" My jaw hurt from how tightly I clenched it.

"You need to come back to me."

"Go." My voice cracked rather than coming out strong.

My apartment door swung open without warning, and Dustin strode in. He walked up to me, wrapped an arm around my waist, dipped his head to mine, and kissed me. He somehow managed sweet and hard at the same time, and I grabbed fistfuls of his shirt, needing something to hold onto, as I pressed back into him.

"Missed you, Addie," he murmured against my mouth when he broke away. He straightened and turned to Sean, never taking his arm off my waist. "Didn't miss you. Something I can do for you?"

Phillip was here too, like I'd magically summoned them both, and he'd moved to my other side, subtly angling himself between me and Sean.

Sean glanced between them before focusing on me again. "I didn't mean to interrupt. Text me and let me know when we can talk."

"Thanks. She won't."

I should be miffed at Dustin for speaking for me, but I was too grateful at Sean's leaving.

The instant he was through the doorway, I closed and bolted it locked behind him, then leaned against it. At least I didn't have to worry now about how awkward it would be seeing Dustin and Phillip again. "Thank you. I'm sorry. I called the first number in my phone. I just wanted to make him leave."

"You don't have to apologize." Dustin's shrug was so casual, it was sexy, especially combined with the growl that lined his voice. "I'm always here for something like this."

"We both are," Phillip said.

I was on board for that. "How did you get here so fast? Both of you? How did you know where *here* was?"

"I have your resume. It's got your address on it," Phillip said.

"We were on our way to breakfast. Lunch? Brunch? Come with us," Dustin offered.

I didn't mind making a habit of spending more time with them, but was that weird?

Phillip jerked his thumb toward the door. "You did say we were taking you out. We can't make you a liar. You'll need to come with us."

I didn't want to stay here, and I did like the idea of their company. "If you insist."

Dustin grasped my fingers and tugged me from the door. "We do. Get whatever you need, and let's go."

I grabbed my stuff, and headed with them out to Dustin's SUV. When I saw Sean's car waiting by mine, him still in the front seat, a sick pit grew in my gut. He took one look at us and peeled out of the parking lot.

What the hell?

11 /
phillip

Despite my resolve last night to put some distance between myself and Dustin, I didn't hesitate this morning when he asked if we were doing breakfast. Then again, he'd dropped everything the instant Adrienne called.

And it was a completely different situation.

I opened the passenger door for Adrienne. "You take the front. I'll call the police."

She took her seat, lips pursed, and I slid into the second row, putting myself between Dustin and Addie so I could see them both.

"What are young going to tell them?" Adrienne asked when I pulled out my phone. "That my ex-husband dropped by my apartment to talk to me?"

Dustin started the truck. "He's stalking you."

"Says you. Says me." Adrienne's voice was tight. "He'll say otherwise."

I hovered my thumb over the keypad, ready to

dial. "It's three against one." It didn't work that way, I knew, but she couldn't let this drop.

She twisted in her seat and covered my hand with hers. "Please don't. I'm not..." She clenched her jaw as she trailed off.

"Not what?"

She puffed out her cheeks and exhaled. "Not in the mood to be told it's nothing, and that maybe I should just hear the guy out."

"Ah." That killed a lot of my replies.

"What are you going to do when he keeps coming back?" Dustin navigated traffic with practiced ease.

Adrienne shrugged. "I'll deal with it. I didn't this time, but I'll figure it out. I'm sorry I made it your problem, but I know it's really on me to handle." She sounded apologetic and distressed.

Neither one felt right.

"He wants to talk, then tell me where he lives and I'll go talk to him," Dustin said.

I understood the sentiment, but also the futility of it.

"That will *not* make things better." Adrienne's answer didn't surprise me.

Dustin turned another corner toward our usual breakfast place. "It might."

She shook her head, but a small laugh escaped. "I can't stay by your side forever, and if you piss him off, he's going to look for a way to make himself feel better. I just want him to go away, and I'll figure it out."

I wanted to tell her ignoring the problem wouldn't make it go away, and I didn't see how it could. But like any troll in any online game or forum, giving him attention wouldn't help either.

"I've got it, I promise," Adrienne said.

I wasn't used to hearing that tone from her. Deception? It couldn't be. I didn't know her well enough to make assumptions, though, and despite all of this, I only needed to know her well enough to teach her how to do my job.

Dustin could stand getting to know her better, though. The two of them worked well together, already, and that dynamic could be enhanced. This morning seemed like the perfect way to nudge their friendship closer, and for me to start stepping back.

That didn't mean I liked dropping the subject of how to help Adrienne with her ex, but I didn't know what to say that hadn't already been said.

We reached the same diner we hit up every other weekend, parked in the same spot, and inside, waved at the same waitress as we sat at the same table as always. When did my life become so inter-twined with Dustin's?

The difference today was Dustin slid in next to Adrienne. They were cute together. A knot formed in my chest and I ignored it.

"Hey, guys." Heather greeted us with her same

friendly smile. "And new friend. Is this your sister?" She looked at Dustin.

I shook my head. "No."

Adrienne was most definitely not Daria. Who I also knew better than seemed normal for co-workers. And I knew her girls too.

"Someone's. Not mine, though." Dustin draped an arm over Adrienne's shoulders.

Adrienne smiled. "We work together."

"You do the games too? That must be a lot of fun. Diet for you." Heather pointed at Dustin. "Coffee, half-and-half." She pointed at me. "And for you?" She asked Adrienne.

"Hmm." Adrienne scrunched her nose in thought.

How was that cute? The kind of tiny detail that made a drawing three dimensional even when it was flat.

"Coffee. Sugar. Do you have the flavored creamers? Any of those. Surprise me," Adrienne said.

"You got it, hon." Heather left to grab our drinks.

I couldn't help but tease Adrienne just a little. "If you don't want to taste the coffee, you shouldn't order the coffee." I kept my tone light.

She stared back, unfazed. "You don't salt your food? It's a flavor enhancer."

"*Oh*." Dustin's face lit up. "Like pineapple juice."

And now breakfast had a cum joke involved. Yup, that was us.

Adrienne's cheeks turned pink. "I'd have to take your word for it."

"You don't *have* to. There are easy ways to find out for yourself." I shouldn't be following this line of conversation. Now that I was thinking about how not-coworker-like Dustin and I were, it was obvious that I was drawn into every joke and jab and bit of innuendo, and that we were dragging Adrienne along for the ride.

Not that anyone seemed to mind. But there was a distinct line between jokes about blowjobs and offering to show someone if myths about pineapple juice making cum taste better were true.

Adrienne drew her finger down the back page of the laminated menu. "Doesn't look like they have pineapple juice on the menu. Bummer."

"Damn. Too bad no one else sells it," Dustin teased.

I wasn't doing this. Because then I'd be tempted to recreate last night, but naked, and *fuck* that was already too tempting. "You know what pineapples always make me think of?"

"South Park?" Adrienne asked.

"Paris Hilton?" Dustin added.

And she got the same references we did. I laughed in spite of myself, but I was still going to make this conversation not sexy. "Xenomorph eggs."

"Gross," Heather said as she passed our drinks to us. She took our food order.

When she was gone, Adrienne said, "I always thought the eggs looked more like... mangoes."

"I was thinking avocado." Dustin scooted the rainbow assortment of flavored creamer closer to her, then took a long drink of his Diet Coke.

Adrienne picked through the flavors, landing on green, and dumped a few into her drink. "They're not bumpy enough to be avocado. Maybe avocado colored mangoes?"

"You've done an extensive study of Xenomorph eggs?" I wasn't impressed. Maybe just a little. I was also just a little tempted to steal one of her flavored creamers. Just one Irish cream.

She raised her eyebrows. "Aliens is classic sci-fi horror. One of the best movies in its class, and one of the few that's stood up to time."

Fuck me, she was a fan. Why couldn't she love, I didn't know, conspiracy theory podcasts? Something completely unappealing. She did have one thing wrong, though.

"You mean Alien," I said.

"No. I mean Aliens. With an S. Don't get me wrong—Alien brought Geiger to the big screen, and... wow. But Aliens is something else."

I could argue that with her, and have a lot of

fun. But I'd rather put the focus back between her and Dustin. "Dustin loves the prequels. The Alien prequels, not like The Phantom Penis."

Adrienne snorted a short laugh. "Like, Prometheus?"

"I don't *love* them. We're just occasional fuck buddies."

She stared at him with a blank expression. Damn, she had that look down. "What does that even mean?"

Dustin shrugged. "I have an appreciation for their more subtle points and sometimes we sneak away into the shadows to do naughty things."

"Like watch them," I said.

"I won't apologize." He never did. Not for his passions.

Adrienne sipped her coffee. "Usually I don't like the term guilty pleasure—who should feel guilty for liking what they like—but *Prometheus*?"

"We'll watch them. Today. I'll teach you how to appreciate them," Dustin said.

Did I really want to push them closer as friends and me onto the outside? Yes, but not today. We were here, we were having fun, and I was going to enjoy it. "I've got a great theater setup at home."

"He really does." Dustin shifted in his seat so he was half-facing Adrienne. "What are you doing with your afternoon, Addie?"

"Apparently, I'm watching the Alien movies."

Dustin high-fived her. "Smart lady."

"And then reminding you when we're done that you're wrong." She grinned.

He scoffed. "As if."

Our food arrived and conversation stuttered as we ate.

"What's the news with that Nolan guy?" I asked Dustin. In the bedlam of the last week, I'd forgotten to get an update.

Dustin sneered. "Rotting in Hell? It's in Legal's hands now. We're clear."

"Who's Nolan?" Adrienne asked.

"Dickhead extraordinaire." Disdain filled Dustin's reply. "But more specifically, a guy I used to work with who's claiming AcesPlayed ripped off his art."

Adrienne looked horrified. "That's... How are you supposed to fight something like that? Why would anyone...? I don't understand. You wouldn't."

She was right—Dustin wouldn't steal someone else's work and neither would I. But her faith in us was reassuring anyway.

"It happens a lot in this industry." I tried to return the favor of being reassuring. "We're lucky that we have lawyers behind us."

"It'll be fine," Dustin said. "It's irritating to be called a thief, and infuriating to be betrayed by someone I used to call *friend*, but we've already handled it."

"You're taking it a lot better than I would." Adrienne didn't sound convinced.

I gently nudged her toe under the table, drawing her attention. "That's because you're not a cold, heartless husk. You still care about the world." The words came out with the playfulness I wanted, but they echoed hollowly inside.

Her smile was warm. "You can't fool me. I know you actually care."

The snippet of conversation echoed in my thoughts, especially Adrienne's confidence in us, and the uncomfortable tug of emotion inside me. Why, after being certain for months, did part of me whisper I'd be losing something incredible if I went through with my quiet plan to quit?

As we were finishing our meal, Adrienne reached past Dustin to grab the check from the edge of the table.

I reached for her, but he got to her first, pinning her wrist to the table. "You'd really wound my masculinity like that?" Dustin sounded somber.

She didn't look impressed. "You'd really tie your masculinity to a restaurant bill?"

"Which answer makes you feel better?" I asked.

Adrienne cast a glance in my direction. "Take a guess."

"Hmm…" Dustin plucked the piece of paper

from her fingers. "I'm paying anyway, because it's my week. You get the next one."

She didn't try to break free of his grip. "I'm holding you to that."

Which meant she and Dustin both planned she'd be here for at least one more breakfast.

The attraction between them was obvious. They might be a cute couple, but more likely they'd be good friends. Dustin wasn't a commitment kind of guy, which was one of the reasons I liked our friendship. Adrienne very much struck me as a settle-down long-term kind of woman.

Though, maybe they'd be the kind of friends Dustin and I were.

That knot was back in my chest. I gulped down the last of my water to wash away the unwelcome feeling.

dustin

It was more fun swapping movie critique and light-hearted barbs with Phillip and Addie than it was watching the movies themselves. But every time the credits rolled or one of them walked across the room, my brain reset and I was treated to memories from last night.

The memory card sat in my computer, and had I jerked off to the replay this morning like it was the best porn ever? Damn straight.

Did that stop me from wanting a redo, but naked and with me in something more intimate than a spectator role?

Not even for a second.

Addie returned from putting a glass in the kitchen, and I wrapped an arm around her waist as she walked past me. She squealed when I tugged her into my lap, but she settled in, rather than trying to get away. Did bald Sigourney Weaver make me horny? No, but these two brilliant, fun people did.

"I've been thinking, you two had all the fun last night." I locked my gaze on hers.

"You were there too." Addie's voice was quiet and sweet.

Heat flowed between us, and her lips were so close. So tempting. I shifted to give her better balance and keep her here longer. "I was *watching*. Which is fine, but if you hadn't noticed, I'm more of a center stage person than an audience person."

She licked her bottom lip. "I might have."

"We could always pick up where we left off." God bless Phillip and his genius.

But I wanted something a *teensy* bit different. "I was thinking more like we rewind and make some revisions."

"Revisions are an important learning tool in art," Addie said. "What did you have in mind?"

I cupped her cheek. "This, for starters." I crushed my mouth to hers.

Somehow she managed both hesitant and hungry as she leaned into me. I sucked her bottom lip in, capturing it between my teeth before letting go.

"Is this okay?" Addie's question was breathless, and she never pulled away. How was she such a tempting dichotomy?

"Do you want to stop?"

"I didn't say that, and no, I don't want to stop."

Another thing I enjoyed immensely about her company—her constant, almost involuntary honesty.

"But we work together," she said.

"True." I was so used to simply hooking up I hadn't stopped to think she wasn't. I should probably make sure she knew what this was. Did I know what it was? Nothing with a commitment attached to it, or that would push her out. "But we're not at work right now, and this has nothing to do with how we do our jobs."

She licked her lips.

When I leaned in to kiss away the shine, her gasp was fuel spilling through my veins.

"I meant, it might help me do mine better," she said.

"See?"

Addie ducked her head. "But what if..."

I tilted her chin back up, needing the eye contact. "What if what?" I kept my tone kind and patient. There was no way she could miss my erection digging into the back of her thigh, but I could try not to be too pushy.

"What if you don't like it and don't want to work with me anymore after?"

I couldn't even fathom. "The possibility never crossed my mind."

"It should have."

I brushed my lips over hers, then leaned in, deepening the kiss until all the raw need flowing between us overrode everything else. "I promise you," I nipped her lips again and again, "that's not going to happen."

"I don't know what I'm doing."

"We do." I kissed her again.

She whimpered against my lips. "Yeah, you really do."

I couldn't fight my smirk, and now I had even more motivation to make sure she enjoyed the hell out of this. I gripped her neck and brushed my lips over hers, again and again. Hard kisses. Soft kisses. They were all fun, especially when she squirmed in my lap. Part of me wanted to be impatient and rush toward the part where the clothes all came off and the soft sighs became loud screams of pleasure. But this anticipation was so sweet, I was going to stay here a bit longer.

Phillip slid a hand between us, gripping Addie's chin and stealing her away to tug her mouth to his. I had a good idea of where her groan came from, because I'd been on the receiving end of that kiss. Watching it play out, knowing what both of them felt in this moment, was scorching.

How had I never been tempted by the idea of a threesome before?

Because there had never been two people I wanted this way at the same time before.

Every bit of last night, watching from behind the camera, joining in, was burned into my memory. Even if I hadn't reviewed the clip a few times this morning, I'd remember it all vividly.

And I was inspired by a moment stolen from time. Hands on her hips, I urged Addie to her feet and turned her so her back was to my chest. I glided a hand down her stomach. "You mentioned something about enjoying the possibilities this presents."

"I definitely did." She arched her back, bringing her hips closer to my hand and her long, tempting neck closer to my mouth.

I ran my lips along the curve, from her shoulder to her ear, sinking into her scent and the soft sighs that drifted from her throat. It was a shame this incredible woman didn't know what it was like to be worshipped, but I could fix that.

Which meant finding that line between drawing this out and making sure she enjoyed every minute. Why was that so important? It wasn't that I was an inconsiderate lay. Everyone got off, and I always wanted the other person to enjoy it as much as I did.

But Addie was different. Fun. Sexy. Smart. Compelling from the moment I saw her, and her actions—her personality—only making her more irresistible with each passing day.

I undid her jeans and pushed them to the ground, leaving her panties in place. Once those came off, the rules would change. As I nibbled and sucked along her shoulder, through her shirt, then nudging fabric aside to taste her skin, she melted into my touch with a series of soft gasps.

I glided one hand up and the other down, teasing her breasts through clothing, whispering my fingers along her thighs, then over her panties. Heat radiated toward my hand. If I pressed harder, gave into the sway of her hips, would I feel dampness seeping through cotton?

Phillip stepped in, knotting his fingers in her hair without disrupting me, and crushing his mouth to hers as he pinned my hand in place. With Adrienne sandwiched between us, it was easier for her to buck into my touch. To squirm and bring her pussy closer to my hand.

She must feel my erection digging into her. I was surprised I could focus on anything else. The stand-up grope was fun, but I wanted to show her more. She whimpered when I moved back, breaking the kiss between her and Phillip.

I brushed my mouth along the edge of her ear. "There's not the right kind of room to maneuver down here. Not unless you want rug burns."

"I might." Her amusement blended with the breathiness of her reply.

Could be fun, but another night. I spun her to face me. "We should take this someplace else."

"What did you have in mind?" There was a wild

anticipation in her eyes that I could try for a century to capture on the page, and never get right. Her lips were swollen and her chest heaved with each desperate breath.

"Bedroom makes the most sense," Phillip said.

Exactly what I was thinking. Before Adrienne could say anything else, I crouched, bringing my shoulder closer to her center, bent her over my shoulder, and stood. My muscles strained as I adjusted, but it was worth it. She let out a delighted squeal, and I was pretty sure I'd never hear a sound like that again without getting hard.

I caveman-carried her into Phillip's room, and deposited her on the bed, relishing her giggles. I pushed a knee between her legs. Her gasp grabbed my cock and jerked, and in return, I pressed in for a kiss, swallowing her groan and sinking into the sensation of her soft, tempting mouth against mine.

Phillip joined us. He'd already lost his shirt, and he nudged me away from Addie long enough to strip mine off as well, before stealing my mouth.

This was the big reason a threesome had never tempted me—it meant another body to give my attention to.

Addie danced her fingers up my chest, while Phillip sucked on my tongue.

Maybe the split didn't matter, as long as we were all in on it. I certainly wasn't willing to walk away now.

The thought held a heavier meaning than I intended, and rather than follow the feeling for an answer, I broke away from Phillip, and turned my attention back to Addie, looking for another taste or fifty.

13 /
adrienne

I t didn't matter that my introduction to Dustin and Phillip was seeing them naked. Sitting between them, both of them shirtless, Dustin's knee pressed close to my mound, was an entirely new experience.

Was I really asking myself this morning if I could do unattached sex? With them? Seemed that way, because the only thing I wanted was to feel every inch of them, in every way possible.

Dustin—hard and sculpted—did everything with so much intensity. That included the way he kissed me, and the low growls that rumbled from his chest when I traced along his skin, following the muscles. He was an artist's dream, and he was definitely part of *my* fantasy.

I trailed over the AcesPlayed tattoo on his bicep, over his shoulder, and along his neck. He caught my wrist, gripping tightly enough to tantalize, and drew two of my fingers into his mouth.

God how did that feel so incredible, especially with him holding my gaze the entire time.

I wanted to follow the lines of Phillip's body, too. Slender and stunning, with patience and skill radiating from the way his touch glided down my back. But I couldn't get to him without breaking free of Dustin, and I wasn't willing to do that.

Dustin kissed along the inside of my wrist, down my arm, to claim my mouth again. Each kiss and touch sent fissures of need pulsing through me. Phillip shoved my shirt up and yanked my bra down, leaving my breasts on display, the charged air teasing my skin.

He kneaded, gently at first, but his touch grew harder and more insistent with each sound I made. Dustin kissed down my collarbone, lower, to circle a nipple with his tongue. When he sucked me into his mouth, I moaned and pressed into him.

He teased and licked and nibbled while Phillip massaged, and pinched my other nipple, rolling it between his fingers. Desire pooled between my legs, aching for attention, but I was too pinned up to do anything except rock between their touches.

Dustin broke away, and cool air met my damp skin with a new shock of sensation. "Lay down," he prompted, even as he and Phillip coaxed and lowered me onto my back.

Phillip pinned my wrists above my head as he knelt next to me, and continued to tease my breasts, but more gently. The alternating contrast between hard and soft drove my senses as wild as everything else they did.

Dustin kissed along my stomach, hooking his fingers in my panties as he moved lower. He tugged the clothing down, and I felt the fabric cling to my damp skin before finally pulling away. I lifted my ass enough for him to remove my underwear.

I was intensely aware of how exposed I was, lying between them, everything on display. "I guess fair's fair." The awkward joke slipped out without my permission, but embarrassment didn't follow. It was so easy to let go and be me with them, even practically naked, my juices coating my inner thighs.

"I don't know…" Dustin's reply made my heart pause, but the way he raked his heated gaze over me kicked it back on and in double time. "I feel like I got the better end of the deal."

Any argument I had vanished when he lifted my foot, and dragged his lips along the ankle, up my calf. His feather-light touch both tickled and intoxicated. He kissed past my knee, lowering my leg and his head as he moved along my inner thigh.

I squirmed with anticipation. When Phillip mimed this last night, I wanted so desperately to feel what it was like to have someone's mouth down there who wanted it to be there. To find out if oral really was this magical, wonderful thing. Dustin licked up my slit, and my body shuddered in surprise and delight.

"Oh God." The exclamation tore from my throat, and my entire body arched, needing to be closer to his touch.

He pressed in deeper, parting my folds with his tongue, gliding along my skin and licking with an enthusiasm that made me feel like dessert. I wanted to grab his head, pull him closer and guide him higher, but when I tried to move, Phillip held my wrists tighter, and pinched one of my nipples hard.

I bucked and squirmed, but I didn't want to be released. My head swam with the multiple sensations. The longer those lasted, the better, and if anyone let up now, I'd be too tempted to finger myself.

Dustin drove his tongue inside me, the penetration making me cry out and grind into his face. The more I shifted under him, the more it seemed to urge him on. He withdrew, but his fingers glided into me instead, as he licked higher.

When he wrapped his mouth around my clit, climax surged in, finally eager for release. He devoured me with the same enthusiasm as he'd used on my nipples, but his hungry attention coaxed my orgasm out longer, harder, keeping on the edge and fuzzing my thoughts until I was lost in the clouds.

I shuddered from the excess of pleasure, but I

didn't want this to end. My body had its own ideas, finally pulling away from his touch. He eased up, finishing with gentle kisses that made me clench with a combination of *too much* and *more, please*.

Phillip let me go, and grabbed Dustin's hand instead. The one that had been half-buried inside me a moment earlier. He drew Dustin's fingers into his mouth, sucking hungrily, then pressing closer to kiss Dustin.

I watched, dazed and breathless, as their tongues intertwined around each other and Dustin's fingers. Their groans as they shared my taste left my mouth dry. How was this so hot?

They finally broke apart, and the world seemed to pause.

I wasn't ready for this to end. I wanted them to get off. I wanted to get off again. "When do you pin me between you and spit roast me?" I asked playfully.

Dustin's smirk was hungry.

Phillip's expression was more guarded. "Have you ever done anal before?"

"No." I'd also never had my pussy eaten until I came, or fucked my co-workers, especially knowing it was just sex. *Really good* sex. "Tonight is a night of firsts."

"This is more something you work your way up to," Phillip said. "And you definitely don't start with double penetration."

"Especially with us," Dustin added.

I raised my brows. "Pretty impressed with yourselves?"

Dustin stood enough to shove the rest of his clothes to the ground, and his cock sprung free, eager and at attention.

I bit my bottom lip. "That's bigger than I remembered." Because I'd seen them naked, but not erect.

"I've heard that before." Dustin grinned, and looked past me. "From you."

Phillip shook his head. "No. I know exactly what I'm getting with you. Thick, cocky, and insatiable."

"Fact," Dustin said.

"Insatiable means we're not done yet, right?" I asked.

Dustin knelt between my legs again, and leaned in, hands resting on the bed on either side of my head. "No, Addie. We're definitely not done yet." His mouth was close enough I felt the heat of his reply. "I fully intend to find out what you feel like wrapped around my cock."

"Okay." My reply escaped on a puff of want.

Phillip reached behind himself, I heard a drawer slide open and closed, and he handed Dustin a small square package.

The tear of foil resummoned any anticipation that had faded with the banter, and I watched as Dustin rolled on the condom.

He glided the head of his cock along my skin, teasing, drawing out the moment. When he nudged my opening, then slid inside, spreading me open with the slow penetration, his groan mixed with mine.

He leaned forward again to rest his hands near my head, and searched my face. "So fucking gorgeous."

Heat flooded my face. I couldn't find a reply, so I wrapped my legs around his hips, and thrust against him, trying to coax out a hard, fast pounding.

Dustin pressed his weight into me, stopping the movement. "You do that, and I won't last."

"You did take your time with me, so fair's fair." I stopped trying to push. Besides, I wanted to feel him inside me longer. Apparently good sex made me greedy for more. I rolled my head to the side, so I could see Phillip. "Are you just going to watch?" I liked that idea as much as anything else, but I wanted him to enjoy himself, too.

He stood long enough to remove the rest of his clothing, then wrapped a fist around his shaft as he knelt on the bed again. "That's the plan. And it's a good plan."

Dustin moved inside me slowly, reaching a languid pace of in and out, and I resisted the impulse to push back for *more now*. I was captivated by watching Phillip stroke himself while he watched us.

If I reached out, I could touch him, but I wanted more. "I want to taste you, Phillip." I covered his hand with mine, measuring the rhythm as he slid up and down his erection, and urging him closer.

He moved in enough to press his cock to my mouth, and I flicked my tongue out, licking away a drop of precum. He moaned and his eyelids fluttered, as I took as much of him in as I could at this angle.

Dustin straightened and pushed my legs higher as he buried himself to the hilt inside me. He paused as Phillip slipped back and forth past my lips.

Dustin pressed a thumb against my clit, and my body jerked away reflexively. He eased up, and moved again more lightly, letting me adjust to the touch against my hyper-sensitive nerves.

He resumed thrusting slowly, teasing me at the same time. This time when orgasm built inside, it didn't offer release. I hovered near the edge, so close, but with that final nudge just out of reach.

"Tell me what you need, Addie." Dustin's voice was coaxing

"I don't know. Just don't stop."

His chuckle was strained, but he focused his touch, circling and rubbing. His cock twitched inside me, and I released a breath I didn't realize I'd been holding, letting out a long cry as pleasure crashed around and through me.

Dustin gripped my thighs, the rough touch drawing out my climax, and any semblance of restraint was gone as he hammered inside me, hard and fast.

Phillip pressed his cock to my lips as much as he slipped away, as he pumped himself.

Dustin's fingers dug into me, and his grunts grew stuttered and uneven. His movement was frantic, jarring me. Every bit of it was delicious. He paused then shuddered with several more thrusts.

The noises Phillip made were just as incredible. He slipped in and out of my mouth again, grunting as white, sticky fluid struck my face.

As both of them slowed to a stop, so did my world. The sounds of us panting overlapped, drawing me back to a pleasant reality.

"Holy wow." I couldn't manage to say anything else.

Dustin's soft smile and Phillip's dry laugh were the perfect response.

The way they pulled off the rest of my clothes and cleaned me up was as tender as the sex had been intense, and it was easy to let them settle in on either side of me. Had I ever been this content? Certainly not after sex, but at all? I didn't know.

I didn't realize I'd dozed off, safe and comfy and content between Dustin and Phillip, until the bed shifted and nudged me away. I watched the shadows lit by outside light as Phillip pulled on his boxers and left the room.

Sleep beckoned, but curiosity was louder. I was experienced at leaving a bed silently, and I climbed out without disturbing Dustin. My panties and T-shirt were on the floor nearby, a discarded reminder of how amazing the night was. I tugged both on. My jeans were in the living room, but both men had seen me completely naked now, and there was no one else in the house. I could walk around without.

As I left the room, I heard the soft *swish* of a sliding door, and followed the sound. I crept out onto the back deck, where Phillip sat at the edge of a pool, his feet dangling over the edge and silently kicking back and forth in the water.

I sat next to him. "You'll get cold." My voice was too loud in the still, even at low volume.

"I keep the water heated. You should be sleeping."

Why did I follow him? I wasn't sure, but I wanted to stay. There was a sadness around him that I wanted to chase away. "I've been an insomniac most of my life." I tentatively immersed my feet to the ankles, relaxing at the warmth that wrapped around me. "It got worse after I was married." I didn't mean to bring up Sean, and I certainly didn't want to talk about him. About the mistakes I'd made with him.

"You deserved better," Phillip said.

"How do you know that?" There were days I wasn't certain—I'd married the guy. I'd stayed with him. I brought it on myself.

"Because most people deserve better, and you're better than most people."

"I could be a really good actress."

He shook his head. "You're way too honest for that. And Cole is a better judge of character than that."

Interesting observation. I didn't want to talk about my mistakes. "So what's *your* flaw." I probably could've phrased that better.

"I'm sure I've got several."

"Our age and single. The world says that means there's something wrong with us. I'm a divorcée. Dustin's a party boy--"

"Don't let Dustin hear you call him that." His voice from behind startled me, but the third-person reference to himself made me smile. He sat on my other side, arm and leg pressed to mine.

I was really liking this whole *Adrienne Sandwich* concept. "Reese called you that, and since the conversation is about stereotypes…"

"I'm a widower. That's my *flaw*." Phillip's reply was quiet, but bitterness lay underneath.

"Oh." I didn't know what I expected, but that wasn't it. "I'm sorry."

He shrugged. "It happened more than a decade ago. Party boy over there is still going."

I wanted to ask for more information, but his tone held a distinct edge of *let's not talk about this*. I leaned into Dustin. "How did *you* get a reputation like that? I'm not judging. You rescued me from that asshole this morning who I stayed married to far longer than I should've, and you didn't throw shade. I am curious, though."

"Part of my job at Rinslet was Vendor Liaison. I like to have a good time when I go out, I'm happy to drink with everyone, and like we said the other night, a lot of people in this industry aren't bar people."

"In other words, people are jealous that Dustin is good in social situations," Phillip said.

And now Dustin's laugh was off as well. I was just jabbing all sorts of nerves tonight. "Well, I don't think you're a party boy, and I like you just fine."

He leaned his weight against me. "Aww. I like you too, Addie." His kindness and sincerity were back. "What about you and the knob who doesn't realize you're *way* out of his league? What's the story there beyond *thank you for not judging me*?"

"Not a misunderstanding in my case. I was just dumb."

"I doubt that," Phillip said.

Yeah, well… "I met him in college. I'd never

had a real boyfriend—yeah, yeah, I know. Who went to college and had never dated before?"

"No one said anything." Dustin was kind.

They didn't need to. I had self-flagellation down. "I'd never had a guy pay that kind of attention to me before. My friends were already married and had kids, and I was at the point where I figured something was wrong with me that I didn't. When he said all the sweet, intense things, including that he was falling in love, I figured he must be right. And then…"

I didn't want to share too many details, because every moment in that relationship was a reminder of how blind I'd been. "Long story short, he wanted what he couldn't have. When we were together, he pushed me away, and when I left, he was desperate to get me back. We went back and forth like that for a couple of years, before I got sick of it and finally walked away."

"In other words, you saw the best in someone, took them at face value, and you regret it?" Dustin asked.

I stared at him, and the painful simplicity of his words reverberated in my skull. "I guess."

"Don't. Rather, I know I can't stop you from feeling what you feel, but it's not your fault he took advantage of who you are."

I wanted so badly to accept what Dustin was saying, but it wasn't that simple.

14 /
phillip

With Dustin and Adrienne gone, my house was empty. The way it should be. The way it had been for years. The way I wanted it, because it was saf—

I cut the thought off before it could finish forming. Sundays were tinkering and housework days. I had people to take care of the lawn and landscaping, but I left the rest for me, to give me something to do with my time.

The pool could probably use cleaning. A glance through the patio doors and I saw afterimages of last night, sitting by the water with Dustin and Adrienne, the mood saying as much as our words.

I used to see ghosts of Jodie out there. How many years had it taken me before I could use the pool again? Leaving it empty, avoiding it at first because the past hurt too much, and then because the habit was there.

It didn't seem right that the first time I cleaned and filled it in years was shortly after Dustin said *you have a pool? Wicked*.

The overlapping memories gnawed at me, and I turned away.

Wandering through the living room brought back more of last night. Not just the sex, though... the last time I'd been with more than one person at once was before I got married.

I raked my fingers through my hair, yanking and trying to physically extract the memories. Since that wasn't practical, I needed to do something else. I grabbed my phone and called Cole.

No answer. Right. Adrienne said something about them going off the grid. I didn't want to leave a startling message, but I needed to convey the point. "Hey, it's Phillip. Long time, no talk. I understand you know Adrienne. When you get back, you need to hook her up with a doorbell cam. She's fine, just a precaution."

That was disturbingly fragmented and weird, but it would have to do. Now she was taken care of, and I could stop worrying about her.

Because losing her would hurt too much.

The thought punched me in the gut and knocked the wind from me. That wasn't right. I barely knew her.

But that was a lie too. I hadn't known her for long, but I knew she wasn't anything like Jodie, the way I originally thought. I knew she was honest, talented, and sexy.

But I also knew I was leaving her behind. Her. Dustin. That wasn't the same as losing someone. I was choosing to follow a different career path. One where I could be teaching more. Helping people like Adrienne—

Really, I'd never met anyone like Adrienne.

And that wasn't helping.

I headed into the basement, where I was painting one wall of what used to be the family room with a large mural of whatever struck my fancy. *Used to be* because I didn't do family anymore. I didn't do attachments. It might work for other people, but it wasn't worth the risk to me.

It hurt too much to lose the love of my life once. I couldn't do it again.

The admission squeezed the breath from my lungs, and I slid to the floor, back against the cold concrete wall.

I didn't like that thought, not at all.

Leaving now, before things got worse, was definitely the right thing to do.

15 /
dustin

I didn't like dropping Addie at her apartment Sunday morning. Not only was yesterday a blast, but I was still concerned about her ex. She assured me she wouldn't be spending much time at her place today, and that Graham would be back, and she had a plan to make things safer.

It wasn't a great answer, but she wouldn't let me argue.

I could sit outside her apartment, see if Sean came back. How much like him did that make me?

While I was making her promise to call me if there were *any* issues at all, my sister called.

Addie headed inside. When I was sure she was safe, I listened to the voicemail from Daria. "I need a huge favor. Joe was supposed to take the girls for the week while I'm in Atlanta. He was *called out of town* at the last minute." Her disdain was obvious, even in the message. "They're set during the day with school and the babysitter, but I need someone to watch them at night. Can they stay with you?"

I rolled my eyes. Not at her—I adored Daria, and my nieces. But her ex-husband... apparently the world was filled with asshole exes. Would I be one now if I'd gotten married? Probably best I never had to find out.

I called her back.

Did my Student Body President, Voted Most Likely to Succeed sister hate going through high school with the same name as a cartoon character who was her opposite? Quite.

Did her divorce teach her to appreciate Cartoon Daria's level of cynicism? Without question.

"Got your message," I said when she answered. "It's no problem, of course."

"Thank you. My flight is in a few hours. Can you pick them up today?" Daria worked for an angel investor firm, and did a specialized kind of on-boarding. She spent a lot of time at client sites making sure they were structured and prepared to take in the investment and use it appropriately.

"Be there in fifteen." I talked to her a bit longer, making sure she was all right and getting an extensive list of instructions that I registered enough so I wouldn't be surprised when she emailed me the exact same thing.

When I got to Daria's house, Harmony answered the door. She was wearing a pink tutu skirt over a nightgown, and she threw her arms around my legs. "Uncle Dustin. *Yay*."

I ruffled her hair. "I hear we're having a sleep-over at my place."

"Because Daddy's a dickhead." She grabbed my hand, tugged me into the living room, and grabbed a tablet off the coffee table. "Come see what I want for my birthday."

I'd correct her on the first statement, Daria would want me to, but Harmony wasn't wrong. And I'd remind her again that her sixth birthday wasn't for three more months, but she'd been planning since the day after her fifth, and wouldn't be dissuaded. I would, however, talk her down from another plan to rent a real castle, if it came up. "Show me."

Harmony scrolled through screens. "Alana says she doesn't want to go to your house. She says it smells like boy."

I had no idea what that meant.

"I did not." Alana's voice came from behind me. She was twelve.

Daria had worked to put Joe through college, and they'd never intended to have a second child. Harmony was a graduation celebration baby. I was pretty sure the pregnancy had been Joe's way to try to keep the marriage together, but I'd never say that. Daria loved both girls dearly, and so did I.

"Don't be liar," Alana said

"I'm not a liar, you're a liar," Harmony screamed.

"*Enough*." I put an edge in my voice to make it boom. I'd spoil these girls from here to the moon and back, but that didn't mean I let them get away with bickering. "I don't care if it was or wasn't said."

"Girls, go put your bags in Dustin's car." Daria joined Alana in the doorway.

Alana scowled and lightly stomped her foot.

"Now," Daria said.

Both girls rushed off.

"What does that mean? My house smells like a boy." I asked Daria.

She smiled through the exhaustion lining her face. "I don't know. Lay off the Axe?"

I scoffed with exaggerated offense. "It's not Axe. It's whatever was on sale and had a store brand on it."

"Yeah, right, Lady Killer. As if you own anything store brand. Thank you so much for doing this at the last minute."

"You know it's never an issue. Everything all right? Harmony told me Daddy was a dickhead."

Daria's smile wilted in a long sigh. "I wish you'd corrected her."

"What makes you think I didn't?"

"She got it from Alana. Joe was supposed to be at her swim meet next week, and now he won't make it. He sent her a new sweater as an apology. Pink."

I winced.

"Yeah." Daria tugged her ponytail forward and chewed on the end. "Harmony co-opted it the instant it hit the floor, and Princess Garibaldi is wearing it now."

I snickered at the name. "Tell me that's a bear."

"It's a duck. I can't believe you let them watch Babylon 5." She didn't sound upset.

"I can't believe you haven't yet. They need to be introduced to the classics early."

Daria shook her head. "I emailed you the list for while I'm gone. Let me know if you have any questions. Don't forget swim practice is at six tomorrow morning, and if you feed them pizza for breakfast, at least make sure they take a multivitamin with it."

I'd done that once, when Alana was seven, and Daria had never let me live it down. "I've got it, I promise."

"Let's go." Harmony was back, grabbing my hand and yanking me toward the door.

Daria crouched to five-year-old height. "Give me hugs."

Both girls hugged and kissed her, they said their goodbyes, and we were on our way.

I totally had this. No problem.

16 /
adrienne

Sunday afternoon, Cole showed up with a toolbox, a peephole, and a doorbell camera. When I asked him why, he told me a mutual friend had called, and that Graham wanted me to go stay with the three of them for a while.

Phillip. "Uh, that wouldn't work for any of us," I said.

"I figured that would be your answer, based on what Phillip told me. But you're always welcome, and since you're going to refuse and be stubborn, this is security."

"It's not stubbornness, it's..." I sighed. "I don't have permission from building management to install any of this stuff.

Cole finished measuring out the spot in the door for the lens, and grabbed a cordless drill. "I took care of it. I also made Graham stay home, so call him while I'm doing this."

I didn't want any of this to spiral because of me. Now Cole was giving up his evening and Graham was worried. I could be upset at Phillip for not backing off when I asked him to, but this was all on me still, for staying with the wrong guy for so long.

I dialed Graham, assured him I was fine, and promised him he'd be the first person I called *if* anything like yesterday morning happened again.

"Adrienne." Graham's voice was hard as we wrapped up the call.

"Yeah?"

"I know why you haven't called the police, but next time don't make me hear this from some guy Cole used to work with. Call me. Track me down. I don't care what I'm doing, I'd rather you interrupt than the alternative."

I was grateful he stayed away from details. My mind was already providing me with plenty of what could happen next if Sean proved to be a bigger problem, and I was doing my best not to fall into that panic, since I still had to live in my apartment. "I promise."

After I hung up with Graham, I tried not to hover while Cole finished up the installation. He gave me a quick tutorial on how to use the doorbell cam, told me the footage was uploading to the cloud, to a server where he could access it if needed, and made me promise to call the police if Sean came back.

"I'm not leaving you here alone, if you don't promise," Cole said.

"Okay, I promise."

He left and I locked everything behind him, checked the new camera many times, and wedged a chair under the front door. Then, for good measure, I stacked my muffin tins and baking pans on the chair.

Anyone wanting to come in would either need my permission, or struggle then make a lot of noise.

I made myself comfortable on the couch. I left the curtains drawn tight and the lights off, and found the tamest, happiest movie I could.

Now that I was home, alone with my brain, there was nothing to do but think, and that would be dangerous.

I bounced between wondering if every voice, creak, and car engine I heard was Sean, and falling into memories of yesterday with Dustin and Phillip.

Maybe I was the kind of person who could do casual sex. Last night was... *wow* and I really wanted to do that again, but this crap with Sean was a stark reminder that I was *not* relationship-ready.

I couldn't even sleep in my own apartment without worrying that my last serious guy might want to do more than *just talk* next time.

Sleep came in bursts all night. I'd doze off on the couch only to be woken up by a door slamming somewhere or a siren or the current movie ending and silence settling into the apartment.

When the clock passed five, I deemed it late— early?— enough to give up on trying to sleep, and get ready for work.

Taking a shower was nerve-racking for the same reasons sleep had been.

The text waiting for me from Luna made me smile and was a relief. *Breakfast? Loading Java?*

I'm in. And more than happy for the excuse to leave my apartment. I would've left early anyway, but now I had a destination.

I reached the coffee shop to find Luna already there with Sonya. I waved, grabbed an iced tea and a chocolate croissant, and joined them, dropping into the chair Luna nudged in my direction.

We exchanged a polite round of *good morning*, and I picked at my breakfast.

"You okay?" Luna asked.

I assumed her question was related to why Cole stopped by last night, and I didn't want to get into it. Sonya was kind, but too many people already knew about the mistake that was my ex-husband. "I'm good."

"She said as though she wasn't really, and she didn't want to talk about it."

I smiled at Sonya's narration. "No, really. I'm good. It was a good weekend. Just not super interesting."

Sonya studied me. "I've never said this before, but you're a *really* bad liar."

Luna smacked her arm lightly.

"I got laid, it was really hot, and my ex-husband is probably stalking me." The truth fell out without my permission.

"*Nice.* That's what I'm talking about." Sonya high-fived me. "Except the stalking thing. *Boo.*"

"I'm so excited to find out the results of last week's beta." Luna's exclamation came out of nowhere.

I stared at her, grateful for the change in subject, but wondering if it could've been more subtle.

Sonya raised her brows. "New topic then. Me too, Luna. As you know, the results will confirm for us whether or not we can move into the next phase as planned." Her delivery was a weird combination of wooden and exaggerated.

"Who talks like that?" I asked through my laugh.

"Every character I've ever written. Or hopefully not." Sonya's incensed tone was exaggerated. "Seriously though, I get it. You don't know me, I don't know you, Adrienne's weekend is off-limits."

"No. Just anything that reminds me of my ex."

Sonya seemed to relax. "I get that. I tuck my trauma away too. But since we're talking work..." She leaned in. "You didn't hear it from me, but

Judith is talking to new investors." Her voice was low.

"Are we short on funds?" I kept my question soft, but concern budded inside. I'd been assured the company was well-funded enough that it would be solvent for quite a while even without a revenue stream... And I already loved it here, even though it had been less than a week.

"Unlikely." Luna didn't sound worried, but then again, she rarely did. "But more money means more staff and more in-game niftiness sooner rather than later."

"Ooh, we have an art insider now." Sonya grinned.

Luna clucked. "We had an insider before. No one is a stranger at Aces."

"Not the same." Sonya turned to me. "Adrienne understands why it's super important we know what cute new outfits are coming, and she'll make sure my orc looks adorably sub."

"I don't know... What's in it for me if I tell?" I teased.

Luna scrunched up her nose in thought. "Free wi-fi?"

"Ooh, I know." Sonya raised her hand. "You can ship any NPC you want with any other, and I'll make it happen."

Something occurred to me. "We have *a lot* of

power, don't we?" Not just the three of us, but this entire company. I knew we were shaping a different direction in gaming, but at this moment it struck home exactly what that meant.

"Isn't it perfect?" Luna asked.

It really was.

We chatted some more while we ate, and pretended to grumble when it was time to cross the street to start the day. With the men I'd had filthy sex with this weekend. Who I was supposed to act perfectly normal around, because they weren't boyfriends, they were friends. Did the light touches go away? Get more intense? Those were there from the start. What about the flirting? The inappropriate innuendo?

I didn't want to lose any of that.

It was a lot easier to say *causal sex is cool* before I had to consider the details outside the bedroom.

I couldn't ignore my nerves as I approached our office. How was this supposed to work?

"Five things you look for in an adult toy store, during a zombie apocalypse?" Phillip's question drifted into the hallway.

The absurdity of the question calmed me a little. I walked into the room to find them at their desks, chairs turned so they faced each other.

"Hey." Phillip gave me a casual smile.

Dustin nodded at me.

Okay. They were cool. I could do cool. I could ignore the voice that wondered if *acting casual* meant we'd never do anything like this weekend again. It didn't matter. It had been casual fun, right?

"Uh… one, a dildo with a suction cup base," Dustin said.

Phillip clucked. "That you wouldn't normally look for."

I couldn't help but laugh, which drew more attention in my direction.

"Let Addie do this one," Dustin said.

My mind froze. "I'm good."

"Come on," Phillip coaxed. "Five things you grab from an adult toy store during a zombie apocalypse."

I had no idea what to say. "Handcuffs." I spat out the first thing that came to mind after *dildos*.

"See? That's smart." Phillips's praise warmed me in a way it probably shouldn't. "Possible one-time use, but if you're close enough to need them, you'll be glad you have them."

Dustin's sigh was exaggerated. "I think you mean *boring*."

"Excuse me?" I looked at him in disbelief. "I think *you* mean *practical*."

"That's one." Phillip ticked off his first finger. "Four more."

I hadn't spent much time in adult toy stores. I'd ordered a few vibrators online, but never dared try anything beyond a bullet vibrator. I racked my brain. "Inflatable sheep."

Dustin grinned. "Better, but you have to justify it."

"If I get lonely and need someone to talk to, I'll feel really awkward talking to an inflatable woman named Ingrid, who never closes her mouth."

"That's two, plus bonus points for the Red Dwarf reference," Phillip said.

"What do bonus points earn me?"

Dustin seemed to consider this. "They're like tickets at the arcade, the more you get, the better the prize."

"How many for another night with the two of you?" Crap. No-filter Adrienne was back. "Thickest, heaviest collar they have." I kept going before either of them could reply. I wasn't sure what answer would be worst—*not an option* or *one*. "Plus, any leather. I'll take a full-on gimp suit if I can find one made of heavier material than latex."

Dustin waggled his eyebrows. "Kinky."

"Anti-bite."

Phillip ticked up a third finger. "Smart. Again. That's three."

Well, shit. What else did they have in places like that? "Flavored whip cream, because you know the world is out of sweets, and stripper heels."

"Nope. Nixing the stripper heels." Phillip shook his head.

Dustin pressed a finger to Phillip's lips. "Shh. Let the lady talk."

"The sheep and I are finally going to learn to walk in ridiculously high heels," I said.

"I'm calling it—four and five," Dustin said.

The laughter faded and we slid into work, but I couldn't erase my smile from the ludicrous game.

I wasn't quite absorbed in my work when Phillip rolled his chair up next to mine. "You ready to implement what you learned this weekend?"

There was my embarrassment.

"Don't do that." Phillip's voice was kind. He leaned in to rest his forearms on his knees. "It was a learning experience. It was also a lot of fun, and just sex." He said it so plainly. So simply.

"So... we pretend it didn't happen?" I wasn't sure what he was getting at specifically.

He shook his head. "We don't pretend anything. Except to be fucking in front of a camera. Just don't be embarrassed by it. Unless you have regrets."

"Most-definitely-not." The words tumbled out before I could consider if that level of enthusiasm was appropriate.

The way his soft smile twitched into place, I'd done fine.

Dustin's phone chimed. "I need to take this. Be right back."

"Now that we have that out of the way, take the scene you were working on last week, and redo the core positions based on what you've learned," Phillip said.

He made it sound simple, but every time I thought about this weekend, heat flooded me and desire thrummed between my legs. I needed to get that under control or my career here would be a series of heated daydreams punctuated with wrecked panties and nothing getting done. "I don't know where to start."

"Pick—do you want to start with the easiest to fix and work your way up, or start with the hardest and get it out of the way?"

"Can I alternate between the two?"

"A little soft and a little rough? Of course." Phillip sat close enough his leg pressed into mine. He reached past me to grab my mouse, and navigated to the files on the network.

Dustin's loud sigh interrupted the moment, and I looked up to see him lean against a nearby table. "I'm watching my nieces while Daria is out of town, and Alana's school just called. I need to take off for a few hours."

How sweet was it that he had stepped into that role so easily? At least, I assumed based on how casually he talked about it.

"Is everything all right?" I asked at the same time Phillip did.

"Yeah, she's just— I guess she got her first period." Dustin finished the sentence quietly.

"First? At her age?" Phillip sounded surprised.

I rolled my eyes. At least they weren't completely shying away from the topic. "Okay, first of all, don't you dare say *anything* like that around her. If she needs supplies—"

"Addie." Dustin focused on me with a grin. "You should come with me."

Nope. "Not even for a friend."

His smile vanished. "We're not friends?"

"I didn't mean— That's not— Of course we are. She already hates that she can't call her mom, I almost guarantee it. If you bring some random stranger—to her—from work because you're embarrassed to help her yourself..." I'd let him finish the thought.

Dustin scrubbed his face, distorting his sigh. "You're right. Because you're brilliant. If she needs *supplies*?"

"She probably already knows what she wants. Take her to the store, let her decide if she wants you there or waiting in the car. If she needs help, don't get the store brand. Regardless of how that goes, make sure she gets a milkshake after."

He raised an eyebrow. "Does that help?"

"For most of the rest of most women's lives," Phillip chimed in with a kind laugh.

God, I liked him.

"All right." Dustin stood straighter, his voice

firm. "I've got this. I'm calling you if I don't." He looked at me again.

I conceded, and he was on his way. I turned back to Phillip's instruction, repeating the mantra *stop thinking about trying this with them.*

It didn't work.

17 /
dustin

I could win over the most stubborn manufacturer in contract negotiations, but I couldn't get my niece to say more than a syllable at a time to me as we drove away from her school. I'd talked to Daria on the way here. She assured me Alana had everything she needed at home, and that she'd be fine alone for a few hours at either her place or mine, while I went back to work.

"If you don't tell me what you want, I'll pick," I said.

She sank lower in her seat, arms crossed. "Fine."

"Milkshakes." That had to be a winner. Phillip and Addie both said so.

"No."

Uh, what? "Then I'll drop you at your house and the babysitter will pick you up when she gets Harmony."

"No." Alana's scowl was etched so deeply it was almost humorous.

Except it was so frustrating. I wasn't used to this from a girl who was usually level-headed and disciplined. "Do you want to change your clothes and go back to school?" I was back to asking. So much for taking a firm stance.

"No."

Daria and Addie both said to give Alana the final say. I was willing to do that, as long as she suggested *anything*. Hopefully it wouldn't be illegal, but I'd consider it at this point. "What do you want to do?" I kept my frustration from my voice.

"It doesn't matter. You won't let me."

"You won't know unless you ask."

"I'm keeping you from work." Her tone shifted in an instant, the anger vanishing, replaced with... guilt?

Was this a hormone mood swing thing? A teenager thing? I had no idea. "What do you need in order to make today better?"

The instant her pout appeared, I'd lost. It didn't matter what came next. I was such a sucker.

"I just don't want to be alone," she said.

That was easy enough. Unless it was followed by *let's go hold up a jewelry store*. "What do you propose?"

"I want to change my clothes, get a brownie and coffee from Loading Java, and stay at your office the rest of the day. I promise I'll be good." Like that, her tone was clear.

I'd totally been manipulated. At least it was a simple request. I believed her that she'd behave, but letting her walk around the office... Sure, our game was 90% like any other game, but that 10% of pure adult content came largely out of my department. I wasn't accidentally exposing my twelve-year-old niece to a gangbang.

We could make it work. I'd claim the empty office for the day—the one that should be mine anyway—and make sure Phillip and Adrienne were cautious. They were doing training, and it could involve the no-nudity variety. "No coffee."

"Mom would let me."

I could see Daria doing that, but I wasn't sitting up all night with a strung-out kid. "Caffeine makes the cramps worse."

"Nuh-uh."

"Google it." I pulled into Daria's driveway. "And while you're doing that, grab what you need and get changed. We'll get brownies and you can stay with me at work."

She clapped and hopped from the car. "Thank you. You're the best uncle ever."

I absolutely was. I followed her inside at a more sedate pace, dialing Phillip as I walked.

"Are you surviving?" He answered.

I chuckled. "I'm managing. I *have* already caved to her demands, though."

"Sucker. Did you give her your credit card and drop her in front of the mall?"

"Pretty sure kids her age don't hang out at the mall, especially not alone."

Phillip clucked. "Fair. What did you agree to?"

I laid out Alana's request.

"Sucker," Phillip said again. "But no worries. Adrienne and I will start concept art for the Christmas event. See you in thirty?"

"Yeah." I nodded as I agreed, even though he couldn't see me.

Alana was the same pleasant, uptight kid I expected when she got back in my car. We stopped for treats and I made sure to get drinks and pastries for Phillip and Adrienne too, as a thank you for changing their work plans for the day.

At the office, we stepped onto the elevator at the same time as Judith. The way she glanced at Alana with a raised eyebrow rankled me. I was glad Alana was focused on her phone and didn't see.

"I know." I kept my response vague on purpose. "I've got it under control."

"If this comes back on us, it's on you." Judith's tone was hard.

Which I was used to. "It won't."

"I promise not to peek at any cartoon tits. Gross." Alana never looked up from her phone.

Judith rolled her eyes.

I laughed. "See? All good."

We reached our floor, and Judith turned to Alana. "Come back in ten years, and you can have a job."

"If I come back in ten years, it'll be for your job," Alana said.

Judith almost smiled. "I'll be waiting." She turned toward her office.

Alana and I headed down a different hallway. I entered the Art room a few feet ahead of her, to make sure everything was clear, but wasn't surprised to see the beginnings of Christmas outfits on screens.

I cleared my throat to announce my presence, then handed out the coffee and such. "Alana, this is Adrienne, she started last week."

"It's lovely to meet you." Adrienne's smile was warm and sincere.

"And you know Phillip," I said.

Pink rushed to Alana's cheeks and she ducked her head. "Hi." Her voice was instantly meek.

That was bad. No more visits to my work for her.

I hid my reaction and pointed her toward the office. "We'll be in there."

It was easy enough to give Alana a corner of my desk to set up on, while I put my laptop on another. The next couple of hours went smoothly as I vetted review sites for content and ensured our press kits were in order for the next stage of our beta.

Alana's phone rang, and she glanced at the screen. "It's my swim coach, can I answer?"

"Sure."

"This is Alana." She was more professional than half the people I'd worked with in the past. "Yes... Of course... That's fine, I understand."

Sweet as sugar.

I turned back to my work. Out of the corner of my eye I saw Alana set her phone on the desk next to her tablet.

And then she let out a high-pitched, ear-splitting scream.

The fuck? "What happened?"

Phillip and Adrienne were in the doorway within seconds. "What's wrong?" Phillip asked.

Alana scowled, crossed her arms over her chest, and sank in her chair. Pink splotches dotted her cheeks. "It's not fair."

"What's not fair? We'll deal with it." I was calm on the surface, despite the mixture of confusion and frustration boiling inside. My phone chimed with a new text.

"Shut up." She glared at me. "You're a stupid boy and you're pretending you understand me and you're a big faking liar and I want Mom."

That deteriorated quickly. I glanced at my phone and the message from Daria.

Alana's swim meet was moved up. I'll be home for it. Don't let her freak out.

I read the message to Alana even as I texted back *Too late*. "See? She knows and it'll be fine."

"It's not fine. This sucks. You suck. It's not fair."

I was already dialing Daria. No answer.

Alana stomped to her feet, and stormed from the room.

"Wait." I rose to go after her. I had no idea what I'd say, but I wasn't leaving her alone.

"Sit." Adrienne stepped in my path, surprising me. "I'll be right back."

Kind of her, but not reassuring. "I've got it."

"Obviously." Her tone was flat. "But let me help."

I dropped into my seat and pinched the bridge of my nose. "At least I didn't let her get the coffee." My weak joke landed flat.

My messenger chimed, I looked at the message from Judith. *Screaming? Glad you have this under control.*

I do, I replied, not sure at all if it was true.

18 /
adrienne

I stepped into the hallway just as the door to the women's bathroom at the end swung shut. That had to be where Alana was.

I'd always wanted kids. Not a big family. One or two. Sean was firmly set against them, and I was grateful now I'd never pushed that issue, but I was also aware my chances for having my own children got slimmer every year.

"Alana?" I asked softly as I stepped into the restroom. The door to the stall against the far wall was closed.

She sniffled. "What?"

"What can I do to help?" I'd been a millisecond from telling Dustin *yes* earlier when he asked me to go with him. It wasn't my place. This probably wasn't either, but no one else was here to do it, and I felt for her.

"No one understands." Her threatening tears were evident in her voice.

Poor kid. "I do. I've never been a competition swimmer, but I used to do dance."

"Really?" She managed flat and sad in the same breath.

"Yes. My first *time* was right before we were supposed to be in a state competition. In all white outfits."

"Oh my God, I would die. Is this some sappy story about how things all turned out okay?"

"Besides the fact that I was terrified the whole time of something going wrong, and the cramps were the absolute worst? Yes." Of course, it was easy to say that almost twenty-five years later, but directly saying *one day this won't matter at all* didn't seem like the best approach.

Alana sighed. "I can't wear pads with a swimsuit."

"When's your meet?"

"Thursday."

"You might not even have to worry about it by then, and if you do, you'll wear tampons." God, I hoped her mother had already talked to her about that. "You have to get used to them if you're swimming." Was I overstepping? Maybe. Did I see another option? Not really.

"Did you win? At state?" Alana asked.

I swallowed my laugh, but didn't have a good response.

"You got your asses kicked, didn't you? Was it your fault?"

I'd be offended by the question, but she was probably projecting her own fear. "No. No. And no," I said. "We were the *good sportsmen there* because we'd tried so hard during the season. But it was one of our best performances ever."

The stall door creaked and Alana stepped out, eyes red and cheeks puffy. "You shouldn't have been there if you weren't good enough."

Maybe. Maybe not. "We showed up and did our best. You have the chance to do the same. You can't lock yourself away for three to five days a month for the next thirty-ish years."

"I guess not." She trudged to the sink and washed her face.

We walked back to the Art room in silence, to find Dustin and Phillip still waiting in the office. Dustin visibly relaxed when he saw us. "What can I do?" he asked.

Alana shook her head. "I'm better."

"I'm glad."

"But Adrienne and Phillip are coming over tonight, right?" Alana asked.

Excuse me what?

"They probably have other plans." Dustin's reply lacked resolve.

Alana pouted, as if on demand. "Please?"

This kid was going to be dangerous as she got older. Did *Uncle Dustin* know he was being played?

"It's not up to me. How about I tell them I'm throwing some steak and chicken on the grill tonight, and leave an open invitation to anyone who wants to attend." Dustin's tone was casual, but his gazed paused on me with a look that was half-pleading, half-desperation, and one hundred percent sexy.

How was I supposed to turn down the chance to spend more time with these two super-hot men I totally shouldn't be drooling over? It wasn't like we were going to get *up* to anything, but that didn't mean I couldn't enjoy their company. And even if Alana was working the system, it seemed like a good idea to offer some extra support. "I mean... if everyone else is going..."

"I'm in," Phillip said.

"Me too." It would be rude to say *no* at this point.

The rest of the workday went more smoothly. As five rolled around, we decided Dustin needed a couple of hours to pick up Harmony and get the girls settled, so Phillip and I agreed to be at his house around seven.

The extra time left me plenty of time to over-think the situation—hell, my entire relationship with both men. Which was exactly what I did as I sifted through my closet looking for that perfect outfit that said *Attractive* without saying *Trying too hard*.

Was this my life now? Did I mind? It wasn't a little better than life with Sean, it was an entirely different universe. Sexy men. Sexy sex. Friendship. Amazing job...

I turned my attention back to my closet. I should probably be telling myself this was a bad idea, but there was too much anticipation at a night out with these guys, even if it was babysitting. Was it bad that I was already addicted to Dustin and Phillip's company?

It couldn't possibly be.

19 /
phillip

I'd relegated this weekend's soar and crash to the back of my mind, and used it as a reminder that I was distancing myself from the people I worked with.

Which was why it was probably a bad idea to agree to meet at Dustin's house tonight. The answer slipped out, though, and it felt rude to take it back.

I arrived at his place the same time as Adrienne, and we knocked together. Usually I'd expect a shout from somewhere in the house of *door's open, come on in*, but Dustin had different rules when his nieces were staying with him, so today he answered the door.

The instant we walked inside, Harmony attached herself to my legs in a tight hug. "Hi Phillip." She stepped back and eyed Adrienne. "Who are you?"

"This is my new co-worker, Addie," Dustin said.

She crouched to eye-level. "I'm Adrienne. Nice to meet you."

"I'm Harmony." The girl shook her hand enthusiastically. "Do you want to color with me?"

And that meant Adrienne had been accepted by both girls. Why did that hit me hard with ambivalence? This wasn't my family.

"Give us a few minutes." Dustin's voice was kind.

Adrienne looked Harmony in the eye. "I'll come find you soon, and then we'll color. I promise."

"Okay. Bye." Harmony headed to the living room.

I'd met both girls several times. When Dustin and I were at Rinslet, he'd bring them to family days, which he planned to include things like face painting, bouncy houses, and other activities his nieces enjoyed.

Aces didn't have family events, but Dustin watched the girls on a regular basis so I'd seen them grow up. He adored them and treated them like I assume he would his own kids. The way I would my daughter if she were still here. Would she be friends with Alana?

The memory and question hit me hard and I shook both aside.

"Harmony is enthusiastic and friendly. I should've warned you." Dustin didn't sound at all apologetic.

Adrienne shook her head with a smile. "So she takes after you? I don't mind."

Though I stood right next to them, I felt like I was watching this entire thing from the outside. Like a glass wall divided me from the rest of the room. Was it because this could be the last time I did this?

"Hi, Phillip." Alana's soft, shy greeting jarred me from the odd thought. I'd seen the behavior in the office too. "Do you want to help me make salad for dinner?"

I was keeping my distance from the crush. Awkward. Wrong. Unappealing. No matter how good a kid she was. "I'm going to help Dustin with the grill. Make sure he doesn't screw anything up."

"I need that kind of supervision," Dustin said with a grin.

Adrienne gestured toward the living room. "You can help Harmony and me color."

Alana rolled her eyes.

"If you promise to do it when no one's looking, you can raid my purse for emergency chocolate," Adrienne said.

Alana huffed, but eyed Adrienne's purse. "Chocolate will make me fat."

Adrienne shouldered her purse.

Alana reached for the bag. "But I'm young and can do extra laps to burn it off. I should help you with that."

"Come color with us." Adrienne led Alana in the same direction Harmony had gone.

Dustin was chuckling while he tugged me outside.

"Chocolate bribes?" I asked as we stopped near the grill. "If you're not careful, she'll take your place." Or mine. The thought hit me hard and soured inside.

Dustin waved a dismissive hand. "I'm not worried. Neither of those girls is above taking chocolate from two people instead of one. Besides, I give better piggyback rides."

"You've got your bases covered." I laughed to smother the out-of-place feeling inside. But it was better than sinking into my other impulse. If I wasn't careful, I'd start to feel comfortable here—playing house—and I didn't want that.

Dustin lay the meat on the grill, then sighed. "I have no idea what Addie likes."

A pair of nice, thick sausages. It didn't feel right to make the joke without her here, and at the same time it felt wrong to say it with the girls in the house. The fuck was wrong with me? "I'll go ask her."

I found Adrienne exactly where I expected, kneeling at the coffee table in the living room with the girls, paper and colored pencils spread out in front of them.

"We're drawing pictures." Harmony didn't look up for her work.

"I see that. Adrienne, Dustin wants to know what kind of meat you want," I said.

She raised her brows as she looked at me, and the corners of her mouth tugged up.

Yeah, that sounded pretty bad in a certain context.

Alana huffed. "Gross."

Harmony swapped one pencil for another. "Alana's a vegetarian."

And I was going to hope that was why she didn't like my question.

Alana hopped to her feet and skipped to me. "Adrienne drew me. What do you think?"

It was a chibi version of Alana, and it was appropriately adorable. I wasn't going to use any language that could be misconstrued. "I think Adrienne is a very talented artist, and we're lucky she works with us anyway."

Pink spread across Adrienne's cheeks. *Stunning*.

"I drew my own pictures." Harmony ran up to me as well. "This one's for you."

"Thank you." I took the drawing. It was two men, one with dark hair, and a thinner one with yellow hair. It wasn't Rembrandt, but considering she was five... "It's fantastic. Tell me about it."

"It's you and Uncle Dustin getting married."

I swallowed my cough, and out of the corner of my eye, I saw Adrienne's smile twitch back.

"You're stupid." Alana huffed and crossed her arms.

"I'm not stupid, you're stupid," Harmony screamed.

Moment ruined. Thank God. "Who has homework?"

"I did mine at the office." Alana sounded smug.

"I don't get homework," Harmony said.

I needed a different distraction for them. "Help me get plates and cups ready, while Adrienne tells Dustin what she wants to eat." I took Harmony's hand, and failed to ignore the surge of pain that came with a tiny person holding onto me.

When Harmony and I reached the kitchen, I set her picture on the counter so we could work.

"No." She climbed on a barstool, and folded the image into a mostly-neat rectangle. "Come here." I moved closer, and she stuffed the picture into my shirt pocket. "Hang it in your office," she said.

"I will. I promise." I patted the drawing.

Dinner was served without further tantrums or screaming. It felt odd sitting around the table like a family. I wanted it to be disconcerting and it was comfortable instead. The conversation strayed from Alana and her swimming to Harmony's birthday party and how she was going to rent a castle.

"Your mom said no castles until you're older," Dustin said.

Harmony scowled. "Like, seven?"

"Like, thirty." Dustin's tone was kind but firm.

Alana made a face. "That's old. Gross."

I'd never been so relieved to be called old and gross in my life—even indirectly.

Dustin stared at her. "You know how old we are, don't you?"

"That's different. You were already old." Alana's logic was hard to argue with.

When dinner was over, the girls were good about cleaning up. Alana rinsed the plates, Harmony put them in the dishwasher, and Dustin started it.

"Who wants to watch *Spirited Away*?" he asked.

Both girls cheered.

I should be excusing myself, not getting sucked into whatever this was. Instead, I headed back to the living room with everyone else, and cooperated as Alana sat me on the couch, and placed Adrienne between Dustin and me, before she made herself comfortable on the floor.

The girls fell asleep before the movie was over. Dustin carried Harmony to a room he had for them in the basement, and Adrienne escorted a barely-awake Alana.

Dustin and Adrienne returned.

"It's getting late. I should get going," I said, like I should have hours ago.

Adrienne frowned. "Yeah." She didn't sound as certain. "Home. Right."

The way she rubbed her fingers together and clenched and unclenched her fist said *anxious* more than it did *reluctant*. She'd looked tired this morning, too. "Did Cole stop by last night?" I asked.

She nodded. "He got everything installed."

"Everything what?" Dustin sounded curious.

"*Someone* called him and said I was having *ex* problems."

I definitely had. "You are."

"I am." Her smile was strained. "And I appreciate it. Cole put in better locks, a doorbell cam, and a way to place emergency calls with a button push. But I'm still on edge." Her voice grew quiet with the final words.

Come back to my place, the offer fought to force its way from my throat. That was a bad idea for so many reasons I refused to name.

"I need to get used to it," Adrienne said. "He's not going to force me out of my place, I just need a little time."

"Are you sure?" Dustin asked.

You can stay with me. Damn it, what was wrong with me? "I'll follow you home and make sure you get inside okay."

Some of her tension seemed to drain away. "I hate to impose, but yes, please and thank you."

"Hey." Dustin grabbed Adrienne's fingers and tugged. "Stay safe. Call us if you need. Anytime."

Her smile grew. "Thanks. See you at work tomorrow."

I drove home behind her, and parked near her in her apartment lot. There was no sign of her ex-husband or his car, but I walked her to her front door anyway. She hesitated before stepping inside.

I was torn between *you'll be okay* and *no, really, come back to my place.*

"Thank you again." Adrienne's soft voice pushed me toward the latter option. "Night." She stepped inside and closed the door between us.

Good.

I let out a long sigh as I walked back to my car. Tonight was normal and still fun. It would be easy to get addicted to that again.

But it hurt badly to lose it the first time. Even years later, an ache still sat in my heart. An empty hole where my past had lived. The odds of the same thing happening to me again—my loved ones being torn away by death—was slim, but there were a lot of ways to lose people.

Dustin and Adrienne were co-workers, not family, and they'd be less soon.

Exactly the way it should be, to keep the chasm in my soul from being torn open wider.

20 /
dustin

It felt weird watching Philip and Adrienne leave on Monday night. The same way it had leaving Phillip's on Sunday morning, but more potent. What else were they supposed to do, though? It wasn't like we could all sleep in the same place night after night.

Tuesday and Wednesday, work was back to normal—as normal as it got around here—after the hectic week of beta testing. Except for one thing I couldn't ignore, no matter how much I wanted to. Phillip spent most of his time with his chair rolled up to Addie's desk, showing her some of the more intricate features of the software we used for rendering.

Which was his job—he was brilliant at training. He'd shown me the ropes a few years back, and several other people at Rinslet, and he was back in his element helping Addie.

Still, watching them, their heads bent close, their quiet voices and laughter filtering to my desk, I struggled to push aside jealousy—of her. Of him—I wasn't sure which was stronger.

"What am I doing wrong?" Addie's exclamation came out of nowhere. She was supposed to be working on two characters having sex in a bar. "I understand the body mechanics, but... Standing up sex can't possibly work for most people, can it? You said the other night— Am I missing something?"

"Standing up sex doesn't work. Not for any length of time." I was careful to hide my amusement, because I also understood her frustration. So many types of media portrayed unrealistic things, how was someone supposed to know if they hadn't experienced it? "I mean, yeah, it can be done, but the muscle control, and the strength, and whether or not it's actually enjoyable... The balance is rarely there."

"You're not looking for standing up sex," Phillip said. "You need one character sitting."

She didn't look convinced. Of what, I wasn't sure. "But... I mean..."

"What?" I prompted kindly.

"A dick just isn't that long," Addie said.

Phillip smiled. "It's all about position and angle. We could show you, if you want."

My pulse cranked to *high* at the proposal of

another *lesson*. I'd make a habit of those in a heartbeat.

"I think I might need one." Addie's tone was serious, but the pink that flushed her cheeks was demure.

Fuck she was sexy.

Phillip grasped her hand. "Office."

Addie didn't move. "Right now?"

"No time like the present," Phillip said.

And I liked the way he thought. "Fair warning —pretty sure we can't do *clothes on* for this one, but we can try, if the idea of doing this *here* is too much." It was turning me on, more the longer I thought about it.

"What if I'm not bothered so much as turned on, and hoping *more* clothes come off, not fewer?" Addie asked.

Phillip leaned his head near hers. "That's my girl."

My jealousy surged back, carried on that single sentence, and I still didn't know who I envied more.

We moved into the office, and I closed and locked the door. I did love the fantasy of someone walking in on us, but there were some things I wasn't willing to risk. This was still fairly public regardless, and the idea of doing this here, now, raced through me with excitement.

"Unlike Dustin, who likes the attention, some-

times I have a thing for watching. And directing."
Phillip nudged Addie toward me and stepped away.

"Pretty sure I know where all the pieces go."
Not that I was complaining as I guided Addie
toward the desk.

Phillip smirked. "This is a learning opportunity,
though."

Addie rested her weight against the desk. "You
make it sound so clinical."

"You've never had fantasies about your teachers?" I pressed closer to settle my hands on her hips.
I swore sparks flowed between us at the contact.

She adjusted her position, her body rubbing
against mine. "Not until the two of you."

She was too much fun. I gripped her hips and
lifted her to sit on the edge of the desk.

"The biggest problem you see on TV," Phillip
said, "for the censors' sake, I'm sure, is none of this
will take place with your pants on because dragging
down your zipper—"

"Doesn't give anyone access to *those* parts of me.
I got that far, thanks." Addie stuck her tongue out
at him.

I slid between her thighs. When she wrapped
her legs around me, pulling me closer, I was
instantly hard.

"I didn't mean to interrupt." Addie's voice was
breathy.

I wasn't in the mood for a play-by-play of what I

should be doing; I wanted a little more freestyle fun. I dragged my nose up the side of Addie's neck, inhaling deeply. "There are a lot of things you can do just like this."

"That's one thing. Not a lot of things." She was playful.

I growled and sucked her neck, biting and nibbling, as I glided my hands up her chest to tease her breasts through her top. Her moans were as delicious as Phillip's soft grunt. I yanked down her camisole, exposing her, and moved my mouth lower, drawing one nipple into my mouth as I kneaded her.

She gasped softly. "You win. Those are all good things."

"Just *good*?" I nipped her skin.

She gasped. "Really, really yummy."

"Do you want to make out for a while, or do you want to prove that position works?" Phillip's dry question was tinged with amusement.

I moved my mouth to Addie's. "I know which I'd prefer." I teased her lips.

"You're the experts. I'm yours to do with as you please."

Fuck. I scooted her off the desk, devouring her mouth and her groans. I made quick work of the zipper and button on her jeans, but the clothing got caught on her shoes.

Her giggles broke the contact between us, and

she kicked off a shoe to get one leg free of her pants. "I'm pretty sure I'm not the only one who needs to be exposed." She undid my jeans.

At the touch of her soft hand around my shaft, I jerked into her touch. *So good.* My jeans hung low on my hips. I found enough brain space to roll on a condom, lifted her onto the desk again, and glided the head of my cock along her slick skin.

Phillip moved in, gripping Addie's chin and drawing her in for a long, hungry kiss. Watching them was a whole different experience as kissing either of them, but just as delicious in its own way.

"So much for directing," I teased.

He turned his attention to me with a tight chuckle, and bit my bottom lip before diving in to crush his mouth to mine. "You were saying?" He growled.

"I was saying... Not a clue."

Phillip pressed back into Addie, working a hand between her and me without breaking us apart, and kneaded her breast while he worked his mouth along her body.

She dragged down his zipper and freed his cock as well.

I nibbled her earlobe. "I like a woman who knows what she wants."

"I don't have a clue." She arched her back with a moan when Phillip slid his hands between her legs, teasing both her and me. "But I'm really enjoying the options. It's like a buffet. I can try a little of this. A *lot* of that..." She tugged Phillip's shaft and his grunt rocked me to my core.

I slowly slid inside her, relishing every inch of penetration, Phillip's fingers brushing me as he teased her clit. It took the last of my restraint to stay still when I was buried to the hilt. I wanted so desperately to move, but then this would be over.

Addie and Phillip fingered and stroked each other, their faces both reflecting their pleasure— mouths slightly parted, eyes fluttering shut. Addie's pussy twitched around my cock, the squeezing growing more frequent and intense with each breath.

When her hand dropped away from Phillip and her gasps became stuttered and laced with whim-pers, I knew she was close. He fisted his cock, stroking hard and fast. She bit her bottom lip, her cries escaping anyway.

I was done holding back, as she came, milking me, I pounded hard and fast. I lost myself in the sensations. The sounds—her whimpers and Phillip's grunts. The tang of need on the tip of my tongue. It all wrapped around me, and I let go of any restraint.

My thoughts fuzzed and I plummeted into plea-sure, orgasm rushing up inside, spilling through me and from me, until stars danced behind my eyelids and climax drained me.

The pounding intensity slowed to a stop. Addie leaned her head against my chest, Phillip rested his on her shoulder, and I settled my forehead on her hair. The only sound in the room was us panting, struggling to catch our breath.

How was this—how were they—so incredible?

"You win." Addie's words were muffled by my shirt. "Your dick is long enough."

I laughed.

"I think that's the most unique way I've ever heard someone say *you're well hung*." Phillip chuckled.

"I'm awesome like that," Addie said.

I kissed the top of her head, reluctant for this moment to end. "You're incredible."

We forced ourselves to go back to work, and the mood stayed light and playful in our room until the end of the day.

Thursday I dropped the girls at their schools with the reminder that their mom would pick them up this afternoon, for Alana's swim meet tonight. I'd have my house to myself until the weekend, when Daria had to get back to her remote work.

An empty home was normal, but the idea didn't sit well with me today.

When Brandon stopped by the Art room in the afternoon and invited us all to his place to watch an early screener of a film festival movie, I didn't know who said *yes* faster—me or Addie.

Which was probably the reason it felt like Phillip took forever to chime in.

Maybe after the movie, we'd head back to my place for another round of *lessons*.

21 /
phillip

I'd hesitated to accept Brandon's invitation. My *no* was right on the tip of my tongue, and then *yes* came out instead.

The night was great—movies with friends, just like it used to be—which left me torn. I was about to give this all up, which was the right decision, so why was it easier to accept *just one more* evening out with Dustin and Adrienne than it was to consider when my final day with the company would be?

I should pick myself up and go. I'd spent as much time with people as without over the last week or so. At Dustin's, with Adrienne, even at my place, which I preferred empty and quiet.

So why was I still here, wrapped up with Adrienne and Dustin even though the movie was over, while Danny and Brandon sat in their own content cocoon, and Reese reclined like a queen on her throne?

I was too entrenched in this. Adrienne was coming up to speed quickly at work, and it was time for me to consider moving up the date I was leaving. Judith was just waiting for my final notice, to make things official. Monday might be that time. Hell, maybe even tomorrow.

Brandon sighed with contentment. "Man, Phillip, I can't believe you're thinking about leaving all of this behind."

"What?" Dustin jerked his head up.

Fuck. Maybe I'd pick that leaving date tonight.

"Oh." Brandon grimaced. "I thought with her here, you would've... Oh."

Told someone besides him and Judith? "Nope."

"Her who?" Adrienne's question was uncertain. "Her me?"

"Leaving what all behind?" Dustin asked.

Brandon clamped his mouth shut.

About a minute too late.

"Adrienne is my replacement." I might as well tell them at this point. "I'm leaving the company."

Dustin stared at me, and the seconds ticked away. "Just like that?" he said. "No, wait, *not* just like that, because Brandon knows. Because that's why you hired Addie. You started this weeks ago. You've been planning this."

"Yes." Half of me rebelled with the straight answer. Telling me to take it back. To reconsider. But Dustin was right—I made up my mind long before this. A moment of awkwardness wouldn't change that this was the right decision.

"But..." Dustin shook his head. "Aces... The game... It's all going to be amazing. It *is* amazing. How could you walk away from that? From... everything?"

The real answer hovered at the edge of my thoughts and felt vaguely like fear. If I reached for it, I'd dive into what I felt last weekend. But I didn't want to admit it to myself. To them. *This way I choose when you're gone.* The accusation in Dustin's glare burned through me, and I hated that as much as the way everyone else was staring at anything but me.

Especially Adrienne, gaze on her hands as she fidgeted with her shirt.

I extracted myself from the comfortable pile of us, and bit back my revulsion at the shocking cold of want that rushed through me when I stood. "You wouldn't understand."

"Fuck you," Dustin said.

Yeah. Not ever again. I turned and walked out of the house.

22 /
adrienne

The heavy cloud hanging in the room when Phillip left was nothing compared to the weight pressing on my heart on Dustin's behalf. On my own. Why did this hurt so badly?

"So, we should go." Dustin nudged me upright as he spoke. "Thanks for tonight." He choked off the words. He'd picked me up because he said Brandon's house was hard to find.

"Sure." Brandon's retort was weak.

I walked to Dustin's car with him, close enough the heat from his arm brushed mine, but feeling a chasm between us at the lack of physical contact. The silence was enough to gag on, and Dustin's blank stare as we got in his SUV made me hurt even more.

He sat there, keys in the ignition, engine off.

"I'm sorry." I had to shatter the quiet. I couldn't

stand it anymore. "I'm not here to take anyone's place. I never—"

"Don't." Dustin squeezed my thigh. The heat of his palm and his tight grip shocked my system. "You've been told, never apologize for being you. Or for being here. Or anything. Don't."

I swallowed past the lump in my throat. "Okay."

Dustin raked his free hand through his hair. "Do you want to come back to my place?"

"I don't want to be your rebound lay." That was a bad reply, even for me. But I didn't know what to do. What to say.

Dustin's laugh was strained. "Not for sex. This is going to sound dumb."

"I doubt it."

"I've had extra people in my house for days, and hearing this... I thought he was a better friend. I thought I was a better friend. I don't..."

...*want to be alone*. That was my answer, whether or not it was his. "Your place sounds good."

The drive to Dustin's was quiet. I kept my window cracked, hoping the cool night air would calm me. It didn't work.

At his house, he showed me to the guest room—which was the same as the photography room, but with the cameras put away—handed me a shirt to sleep in, and told me *good night*.

I wasn't sure what I expected, but this wasn't it. An ache set in my chest from what I witnessed at

Brandon's, between Dustin and Phillip. I hadn't imagined Dustin's hurt. Or how fake Phillip's indifference was. "Do you want to talk?" I asked.

"About what? Not *him*."

That wasn't a good sign. "Something else, then. If you go to bed now, you'll be up all night stewing about things."

"Most likely."

"I can't make you talk to me, but I'm here if you want."

He shook his head. "You're welcome to the shower, towels are in the closet, kitchen is yours, make yourself at home."

"Thanks." The people in my life would be impressed. Something had knocked the words out of me.

Dustin turned away and disappeared into a room across the hall and one door down.

How fucked up was tonight? It felt weird being in this room again, considering the first time I was here. It felt weird missing Phillip, though he wasn't gone yet. It felt weird stepping into someone else's shower.

The need to rinse off the hurt and disappointment before I fell asleep—like sleep was going to happen—won out over awkwardness. I cleaned up quickly, and changed into the shirt and shorts Dustin gave me. I pulled the drawstring tight, and managed to get the bottoms to hang on my hips.

I could scroll social media, see if that put me to sleep. Play a mobile game? Head into the living room and watch TV? That definitely felt weird.

Before I could decide, there was a knock, and I opened the door to Dustin. His hair was damp, he was only wearing a pair of sweats, and he smelled like soap.

He cupped my face between his palms and crushed his mouth to mine, stealing my thoughts and my breath and my anchor to reason. This felt so incredible. I wanted him desperately, before now, but especially after what we'd done in the office...

I pressed my palm to his chest, barely aware of the gesture until I pushed him back with a *no*.

Someone could let me off this emotional roller coaster now, please, while it was cresting a peak again.

Dustin's growl made my flames of need surge, but he stepped back, breaking the contact between us. "You're right." He scrubbed his face, sat on the bed, and patted the mattress next to him.

I sat, keeping some distance between us, but not much. What now?

Silence again, apparently.

"Why art? What made you pick up a pencil and say *I'm going to get better at drawing*?" Dustin's question was so random, so far away from the core of whatever this mess was, I almost smiled through the sadness, frustration, and confusion.

"This may surprise you, but I'm not always the best at expressing myself through words."

"I find that hard to believe." His tone was sincere.

I ducked my head. "Not everyone appreciates my... quirks." Which I didn't really have to think about around him. Or Phillip. The fallout from the fight at Brandon's would fade, right? Things would be better in the morning? "The drawing started as an outlet, and it made me so happy, I kept doing it. What about you?"

"Nothing nearly so noble."

This conversation, this moment, was surreal. A bubble of peace in the middle of a storm. "My reasons are hardly noble."

Dustin smirked. "I liked drawing dicks on things."

I laughed in spite of myself.

He joined in with a light chuckle. "Told you. I had an art teacher who said if I was going to do that, I should at least learn to do it right."

"Did your parents know?" Me, with my conservative upbringing, couldn't fathom being encouraged at a young age to draw genitalia.

"Knew. Encouraged it. As long as what I was doing wasn't sexual, they were proud of me for being adult enough to handle nude drawing."

I studied him with skepticism. "It was sexual."

Dustin shrugged. "I was fifteen. It was *completely*

sexual. But only until the novelty of drawing dicks wore off. Then my interest was real, and I was good. I wanted to be the best."

"You're pretty amazing." I should qualify that. "At drawing." And other things. "And other things."

He covered my hand with his, and warmth wrapped around me. "I'm not the best yet," he said. "But there's still time."

His confidence was so sexy. Then again, most things about him were. Same for Phillip.

Now the ache was back. I'd only known these men for a few weeks. Was I letting the physical override common sense? Maybe, but it didn't feel like it.

I just didn't know what it felt like instead, or where to start untangling everything churning inside me.

We kept talking, and I didn't realize I'd fallen asleep until I woke up with Dustin wrapped around me. This was so comforting and right.

"Too early," Dustin mumbled against my back.

It really was. Sadness whispered through me as his fight with Phillip rushed back, but it was sandwiched between two wonderful moments. Dustin and Phillip would be okay today, right? This was the kind of thing they could talk through and things would be all right?

Why did it matter so much to me? It was their argument.

But it did matter, even if I couldn't put the *why* into words.

The mattress shifted as Dustin sat up. "Yesterday was amazing," his voice was heavy with sleep and the huskiness was enticing. "The sex at the office, but also talking last night."

No mention of Phillip.

"I'll drop you at home so you can get ready, and meet you at the office," Dustin said.

"Sounds good."

We got dressed and we were on our way.

I couldn't handle another drive full of silence. Not with my brain bursting to capacity with questions. "What are we?" My question tumbled out without a point of reference.

Dustin drummed a thumb on the steering wheel. "People? Skin sacks full of water?"

"Friends? Co-workers? Lovers?" I hadn't lost the ability to be painfully direct and blunt. Go, me.

"Every day at work is a struggle to prove my credibility. A former co-worker is accusing me of plagiarism. I just found out the person I thought was in this with me through everything, one of my closest friends, was keeping a massive secret... I don't know if you want to hold any of those labels," Dustin said. "I don't know much of anything right now. Except that you probably aren't capable of lying to me."

There was that.

Dustin pulled up in front of my apartment building. He squeezed my hand before I climbed out of the SUV. "See you at the office."

I nodded and forced a smile, then headed inside. I rushed through my morning routine, and headed into the office. Dustin was already there, no surprise, and he looked up from his work long enough to give me a weak smile.

Phillip arrived a short while later, announcing himself with a *hey*.

Dustin scowled and pushed back from his desk, managing to make rolling wheels squeal on linoleum. "I have some calls to make." He headed into the vacant office and shut the door behind himself.

So much for everything being better this morning.

"I'll give him some time to cool off, then talk to him," Phillip said.

Apologize? It wasn't my place to correct him, so I nodded.

23 /
dustin

Should this bother me so much? Co-workers came and went all the time. So did fuck buddies. My lack of a long-term relationship history, and job history, spoke to both.

But Phillip was a friend. Or I thought he was. I didn't understand his desire to move on, but I didn't hold it against him.

Maybe a little.

That wasn't the issue either, though.

I'd managed to avoid thinking about this all night, thanks to Addie's company. But now that we were back in the office, seeing Phillip again...

The fury and betrayal were back.

And what he'd done was a betrayal. This wasn't a matter of *oh, I forgot to mention...* Phillip actively made sure I didn't know what he was doing. Why Addie was really hired. He made it a point to deceive me. He lied to me, and I had no idea why.

Was I doing the same to Addie? Her question *what are we* circled in my thoughts, along with every-thing else.

I'd been honest with her about not having an answer, but I was also having a hard time seeing past other people's lies and it wasn't fair to reflect that back at her. I did want her.

As more than a co-worker-slash-friend?

I didn't know. The sex was incredible and so was her company.

Those things were amazing with Phillip too.

Damn it. I pinched the bridge of my nose, but the gesture didn't cut off the rambling thoughts.

My messenger pinged with a new note. Right, I should be working.

Give me a call when you have a minute, Judith typed.

I picked up the desk phone. No reason to keep the boss waiting if I could avoid it, especially since I needed her to see I was the right guy for the job I wanted.

"Getting awfully used to that office, aren't you?" She answered.

The different extension would show on her phone, the way hers did on mine. "The office that should be mine? Yes."

The noise she made was as much huff as laugh. "No. Especially not right at this moment."

"Oh?" I couldn't find a better response that would still hide my irritation.

"Your *friend* Mr. Toph, has sent a follow-up response to his Cease and Desist. He's informed me he'll drop the matter, and not take things public, if we hire him."

I snorted with disbelief. Was he fucking kidding? "Does he think this is some weak Hollywood movie?"

"I'd rather not speculate about what or how he thinks," Judith said. "I'd rather we had a way to shut him down instantly."

"You and me both. I thought we sicced Legal on him?" Obviously it wasn't enough. "Give me some time to think about it, and I'll get you an answer," I said. While I wasn't the one causing the problem, it was happening here, to this company, because I was the person he knew. I'd come up with a solution.

Judith was silent so long I almost asked if she was still there. "You have until end of day Monday," she said.

"Got it. I'll have something for you." I had no idea what, but this gave me the entire weekend and then some to let the thought simmer.

My messenger popped again, this time with a note from Phillip.

In fact, I could spend the next couple of days stewing on the odds of two people I trusted so completely betraying me. I closed Phillip's message without reading it.

Was I being childish? It was possible. Did I care?

Not anymore than Phillip did when he decided he needed to hide the fact that he was leaving. Not anymore than Nolan did when he manipulated me and stole my work.

But that was the problem—I did care, and I didn't like how much it hurt.

I managed to avoid contact with Phillip the rest of the day. Not a practical thing going forward, especially if I wanted to be the boss, but he wouldn't be here long enough for it to matter.

Daria invited me to dinner that night at Buck E. Cheese. Which meant she wanted to apologize to the girls for the last-minute business travel, and she wanted a second set of eyes there to help watch them.

I was fine with that, but surprised with the location. "I thought Alana was too old for Buck E. Cheese."

"It was her request," Daria said. "She told me she had to enjoy it before she was old and gross."

That sounded right.

We picked a table with a clear view of both the ball pit and the arcade, depending on which direction one was facing. The rule was, the girls had to eat at least one slice of pizza before they played games.

Harmony ran off to jump in the pit, and I handed Alana a twenty for tokens. Daria raised her eyebrows, but didn't say anything.

"Who's Addie?" Daria asked when the girls were both out of hearing range.

The question tugged at so much more confusion than Daria probably meant it to. "New woman at work," I said, my attention focused on Alana wandering between video game machines. Was I a proud uncle when she stopped at the Star Wars game? Damn straight.

"Uh huh." Daria didn't sound convinced. "Alana told me that if Joe and I both had to work during her next swim meet, it was okay. Adrienne would take her."

I glanced at Daria, one eyebrow raised, before turning my attention back to the arcade. "Wonder where she got that from."

"I have this tiny nagging fear that never goes away." Uncertainty slipped into Daria's voice. "That whoever Joe's new girlfriend is, they'll like her better than me. It's silly, I know. But the fear is there. I didn't expect them to replace me with *your* girl-friend." Her laugh landed flat.

"She's not..." The denial died in my throat.

"*Mommy, Uncle Dustin,* watch." Harmony's shout carried above all the other screaming kids.

I turned to see her hop into one of the larger slides and squeal as she flew into the pit of colorful balls. Daria and I both cheered, and Harmony looked satisfied.

"Does Phillip know?" Daria asked.

Not who I wanted to be discussing. "Know... Adrienne?" *Intimately*. "She works with us. With me. He's leaving." My bitterness leaked into the words.

Alana skipped back to me and held out her hand. "Can I have money for skeeball?"

"What happened to the other money he gave you?" Daria asked.

Alana shoved her hands in her pockets and stared at her shoes. "I spent it on Star Wars."

"You spent a couple bucks on Star Wars. You pocketed the rest." I'd taken my eyes off her for a minute or two, but not twenty-bucks-in-quarters minutes.

Alana scowled.

"Stop trying to fleece Dustin, and apologize for lying," Daria said.

I stared at Alana expectantly.

She huffed. "I didn't—"

I raised my brows.

She slouched. "I'm sorry."

"Don't do it again. Go play." I waved her off. Best she learn the lesson now, and not when she was *old and gross*.

"So, you and Phillip..." Daria trailed off. "I just..."

So much for avoiding that topic. "Might as well finish the thought."

"I keep wondering when the two of you are

going to figure out how good you are together, and stop pretending you're just friends."

The words slammed into me harder than was fair, and I didn't care for the knot they left in my chest. "We're not even that."

"Okay. Sure." She didn't sound convinced. "Listen, I know I give you a lot of shit about, well, everything. I mean, you're my big brother, I'm supposed to. But there's no one I trust more with the girls."

"I— Where did that come from?"

"I don't know. It just felt like you needed to hear it."

"Thanks." Rather than helping me add some order to my thoughts, they were in more of a jumble now than ever.

24 /
phillip

Saturday morning came and went without a friendly call from Dustin, asking if I wanted to get brunch. Not that we did so every weekend, but today there was no mistaking the reason for the non-existent call. Especially after he ignored all my attempts to talk to him yesterday.

This was exactly what I thought would happen. Dustin found out I was leaving and now he wasn't speaking to me. I understood how passionate he was about AcesPlayed—how much the game and the company meant to him —but the vision didn't hold the same meaning to me.

How was I supposed to explain that to him, though? How was I supposed to make him see it wasn't about him or disagreeing with his decisions, it was simply time for me to move on. There hadn't been a way to avoid this.

Except being honest with Dustin. Not deciding to cut him and Adrienne out of my life.

I didn't like the nagging, insistent voice in my head. It was a little late to find stupid reasons to try to make myself feel guilty. This was the choice I needed to make.

Because I'm terrified.

Nope. Wasn't indulging those thoughts. The opportunity in front of me was incredible and thinking about it—about teaching new people and helping them grow—didn't fill me with anything but excitement and anticipation.

There was no fear or dread associated with the idea.

I gathered my clothes from the hamper to do laundry for the week, and something tumbled from the pile. The instant I saw the folded rectangle, a stone landed in my gut. It was Harmony's drawing. *You and Uncle Dustin getting married.*

Fuck. The memory gnawed at me.

I couldn't throw the drawing out, but I couldn't look at it either. I set it on my nightstand, and hauled my clothes down to the washer.

When I returned to my bedroom, the folded drawing glared at me, far brighter than it should be, and sent fissures of restlessness through me. My fingers itched toward my back pocket, where my phone was. I wanted to call Dustin. Adrienne.

How did she become a part of my life so

quickly? I didn't have an urge to call Brandon, or anyone else from work, but Adrienne hovered at the front of my thoughts, along with Dustin.

I grabbed my phone and dialed Scarlet instead. She was my contact for the teaching position at the university. She wouldn't do the hiring or make any of those decisions, but she had put me in touch with the Dean and kept me apprised of anything I needed to know while I put my plan in motion.

"Morning," she answered quickly, and the smile in her voice was obvious. "You call to volunteer for another drawing class?"

That seemed like a lifetime ago. Had it really been less than two weeks? "Probably not a good idea."

"No? I got a lot of good feedback from the students. I didn't mind the view either."

The light teasing should put me at ease. "It might be harder for them to take a professor seriously if they keep seeing me naked."

"Hmm... Fair point."

"Speaking of"—might as well get to my real reason for calling since we were on the topic—"you said when I have a date for leaving, you'd talk to the Dean about next steps. Let's set it up."

She let out a long hiss. "About that..." The cheer faded from her voice.

Not a great sign. "What's up?"

"I'm hearing rumors, and if I've heard them,

others will too. I don't think you should pursue this job until you clear things up in your current one."

There were problems in my current job? Besides Dustin being pissed off at me? "Clear what things up?"

"These days we lean heavily into how to avoid copyright infringement and plagiarism claims. We have to. If you're a part of something like that, if you're working for a company who's been accused of that, even if it's not your fault, it's not going to reflect well on you."

Fuck. Dustin was supposed to take care of that. Not that I blamed him—the accusations weren't his and I didn't think for a moment he'd done what he was accused of. But if this kept me out of a job— What? "If it hasn't gone away yet, I know it's in the process. But expect to hear back from me when I confirm."

"Totally. I'm here when you've got proof that it's not an issue. Talk to you then," Scarlet said.

Proof wouldn't be a problem, but I'd have to talk to Dustin to get details. I'd burned that bridge.

The thought—the phrase—hit me harder than Scarlet telling me I may not be able to teach. It was a punch in the gut to admit Dustin may never speak to me again.

My gaze landed on Harmony's drawing once more, and I unfolded it, tension cranking through me. I smoothed the paper flat. *You and Uncle Dustin getting married*. I couldn't ignore the knot in my chest. *This* was what I wanted to avoid.

A reality that hit me harder than any others. This raw pain of loss. It wasn't as painful as it could be, the agony wasn't as bad as if I'd let things go on longer with Dustin, with Adrienne.

It was a good thing I was severing ties.

So why was part of me screaming to not walk away?

Because it hurt. That was the only reason.

My phone rang and I clicked *Answer* without pause. It was probably Scarlet. "Hey."

"Phillip?" Adrienne's voice was tiny.

"Are you all right?"

"Yeah. I mean no, but yeah. I'm sorry to bother you," she said. "I couldn't get a hold of anyone else."

All my other thoughts vanished behind concern. "It's fine. What's up?"

"I keep swearing I see Sean out in the parking lot, and I know he's not, that I'm being paranoid, but... God, this sounds stupid."

Not after what Sean had already done to her. "Not at all. Do you want me to come over?"

"No. Yes. Please?"

"I'll be right there," I assured her.

25 /
adrienne

I managed to avoid sleeping in my own apartment most nights this week, and when I was here, nothing bad happened. The stress at work yesterday must have carried over into my paranoia, though, because all night long I woke up at every little sound. Morning wasn't much better. I went out for coffee, breakfast, and groceries, but then I had to come home to put it all away.

The note slipped under my door was scrawled in Sean's familiar handwriting on the back of half a utility bill, and said *Does your 'boyfriend' know how many places you sleep that aren't here?*

Oh, God. Bile rose in my throat and I almost emptied the contents of my stomach right there.

By the time afternoon rolled around, I was jumping at everything. I couldn't get a hold of Graham. Or Luna. Or Cole. Dustin was with his nieces. Why didn't I have more friends?

For the same reason I couldn't sit still now—my ex-husband was an asshole.

I was probably being dumb, but I didn't want to be alone.

There were dozens of other numbers in my phone, but most were people I'd alienated long ago. Phillip, though... He'd said he didn't mind if I bothered him with things like this. I liked thinking about him anyway, but having him here to protect me was too tempting. Still, I was surprised that he said he'd come over—not because he'd ever given me any reason to do anything other than enjoy his company and drool over him, but he was more removed than Dustin, and probably wouldn't be around much longer.

I understood why Dustin was mad at him, but I didn't know Phillip well enough to feel that same sense of betrayal. And he was a million times better than Sean.

A text came through a short while after I called Phillip, saying he was here and heading up. Which made the knock a moment later more reassuring than startling. I checked the camera and peephole anyway, making sure they agreed with each other that it was Phillip on my landing.

I let him in with a grateful smile and locked the door behind him. "Thank you. Again. I just... I'm sorry to bother you on the weekend."

"Don't apologize. I meant it when I said you

could call anytime. For anything, but especially this."

"For now."

"Don't you start, please."

"I'm not *starting* anything," I said. "I'm clarifying. You're leaving soon, right? You don't need some random woman you knew for less than a month calling you once you're gone." I felt bad enough bothering him today, regardless of his assurances, I wasn't calling him when we didn't work together anymore.

A shadow passed over Phillip's face, then vanished behind a kind but otherwise blank mask again. "I meant anytime."

Sure.

This was awkward. How was it things had never been super uncomfortable with him until now? I gestured to the couch. "Do you want to sit? Something to drink? I have water and coffee."

"I shouldn't have more coffee today." He did take a seat, though.

I took the spot next to him—there wasn't really anywhere else to settle in the room. What now? I wanted to tell him not to quit his job, though I didn't have a good reason for it beyond *I like working with you.* No, that wasn't true. I liked him. I didn't want him gone. I also wanted him to make things right with Dustin.

None of those things were my place to say.

"Don't quit. I like having you there. So does Dustin, that's why he's upset. Tell him you're sorry, and stay. I probably don't have any right to ask, but I'm doing it anyway."

His smile didn't reach his eyes. "You're fine to ask, but I can't."

"Oh." I didn't try to hide my disappointment. "Why not? Why are you leaving? Are things bad at AcesPlayed? Do I need to be worried there's something going on I don't see?"

"That's a lot of questions. There's nothing bad at AcesPlayed that I'm aware of. A few assholes, but you're all great at your jobs, and I expect you will make this game into something epic."

I flushed that he included me in the statement, but he didn't answer the question I most wanted him to. "So then why?"

"It's time for me to move on."

That wasn't right. Not because I disliked the answer—though I did—but it felt off. "You were with the same people for almost two decades. I realize Cord, Rinslet, and AcesPlayed are different companies, but they're the same people. You just woke up one day and decided *I'm done*?"

Phillip leaned forward to rest his forearms on his thighs. "No, but also yes. I love the art, but I love teaching and mentoring just as much, if not more. My chances to do that have evaporated here."

You still have a lot to teach me. The words died in

my throat. After Sean, I swore I'd never beg or demean myself or change to keep someone in my life. There it was, the one thing that kept me from blurting out the thoughts in my head. "I see."

Phillip straightened and looked at me, his brows furrowed. He sighed and flopped back on the couch. "You caught my attention that first night in the drawing class. The reason we had a sketch of you for the employee avatars was because I drew you after the modeling session was over."

How was I supposed to respond to that? Elation? Feeling flattered? His tone didn't imply I should be either of those things... or really much of anything at all. So I settled for, "oh?"

"You reminded me of my wife."

The dead one. That sounded cold, but what was I supposed to say? Did he see a ghost when he looked at me? "Oh." Wow, I was witty this afternoon.

"I know how that sounds. It's not that I see her when I look at you, but your focus that night, the way you held yourself... But you're not a replacement for a memory. I look at you, I see Adrienne. And I finally figured out, you remind me of her because like her, you see the world through your own, unique lens. It's in your art, it's in the things you say and do, and it's at the core of who you are."

I still didn't know how to respond. "Why are you telling me this?"

"Every time you apologize for being you, for taking up space, I cringe, because no one should do that, but especially not you. I want to beat the shit out your ex-husband for making you think that was necessary. For making you afraid to be alone in your own apartment on a Saturday afternoon."

How did he do that? Crawl inside my head and know exactly what to say, but at the same time be so clueless about other things, like that it was a bad idea to lie to Dustin about leaving Aces.

My phone rang, shattering the strange mood in the room. I glanced at the screen. "It's Graham." I pressed *Answer*. "Hey," I greeted my brother.

"I was in a movie. Are you okay?"

The conversation with Phillip was odd, but sitting next to him, his arm and thigh pressed against me, I felt safe. "I freaked out a little, but I'm better now."

"A little?" Graham chuckled. "You called each of us at least three times."

Right. "It's dumb, but I couldn't shake the feeling Sean was out there."

"That's not dumb. Not after what he's been pulling," Graham said. "I don't want you staying there tonight."

Me neither.

"I've got it covered," Phillip said.

Could he hear the conversation? Possibly. He was sitting pretty close.

"Sounds good." Graham's response implied he heard Phillip as well. "I'll keep my phone nearby if you need anything."

"Thank you." I disconnected, not knowing how to feel about the exchange. Some guy basically told my brother I was sleeping over. Sure, I was in my thirties, and it was a little late in life for that kind of propriety, but until Graham found Luna and Cole, we barely talked about relationships in our family, let alone alluded to there being a physical aspect.

Unless I counted the number of times my parents asked me when I was going to find a nice man and give them grandbabies.

"Pack a bag." Phillip interrupted the thought. "You're staying at my place until we get this figured out."

We? My frustration welled. "I won't let Sean push me out of my apartment. The place I had to get because he forced me out of my house. I'm tired of him, of anyone else, determining the direction of my life." Except I didn't want to be here. Didn't feel safe here.

"You're not staying here or alone tonight." Phillip stood and tugged me to my feet. "This isn't permanent but I need you safe."

The sudden movement stole my balance and I landed with my face inches from his. My breath caught at the intensity in his gaze. He had such gorgeous eyes—brown with flecks of gold and grief.

He brushed a thumb along my cheekbone. "You'll figure this out—we will. If you need a sounding board. Anything. We'll stay here, if you prefer. Tell me where you feel safest."

"Not here."

I need you safe, the words echoed in my head as I grabbed a couple of days' worth of clothes, and toiletries, and shoved it all in a bag.

When did I lose control of my life? Or had I ever really had it?

26 /
phillip

Having someone else in my house, knowing she was staying longer than a few hours, didn't feel like the intrusion I expected. Then again, neither did having Adrienne here the other night.

It wasn't just the sex, it was the company—the movie marathon that brought us here last week, the late night chat by the pool... Really everything about her had me captivated.

It would be weird if Dustin was never here again, though. I was okay with the idea a couple of months ago, when I made the decision to leave Aces. I needed to get back to that place, but every time I tried, I remembered how right it felt to spend time with Dustin. How much I enjoyed his company. How it was instinct for me to do whatever he asked whenever he wanted, and how he did the same for me.

I showed Adrienne to the guest room. "You can

leave your bag in here." I wanted her in my room, instead. Longer than for the night or the weekend. I shoved the jarring thought out of my head. I was helping out a friend. Nothing more.

"Thanks." Her laugh was dry. "I think I've spent more time in guest rooms in the last few weeks than the entire rest of my life."

And it wasn't her fault. That wasn't right on so many levels.

"How about I grab us some sodas and we sit by the pool," I said. Not the best way to put last weekend out of my thoughts, but I wanted her company, not just a warm body in the house.

Her grin was worth it. "I feel so spoiled, hanging out with someone who has a pool. If it was me, I'd be out there every day I could, dangling my feet in the water, soaking up the sun, and doing whatever."

"Now's your chance to live the dream."

We left our shoes by the back door, picked a spot that would stay half-shade, half-sun for the rest of the afternoon, and dipped our bare feet in the pool.

The conversation came easily, like I expected with Adrienne. We fed each other a series of rapid-fire questions: *Where did you grow up? Favorite color? Best concert ever? Worst movie ever?*

It was simple and perfect.

So when Adrienne said, "Five things you grab very first in a zombie apocalypse."

I replied with, "a way to find everyone," without thinking. Wait. What did I mean by that?

"Everyone who?" she asked.

I didn't… "Everyone." Brilliant. Not.

"The entire world?" Her question was teasing lined with insistence.

If I drew this out, my answer would seem like a big deal and it wasn't. "Dustin. You. Brandon and Danny. Reese would be brutal in a zombie apocalypse."

"I do like her. What else?" Adrienne's smile was warmer than the fading sunshine.

So glad she didn't push the issue, but moving on didn't stop my answer from rattling around in my head. "That's five plus me, right? We'd make the most kick-ass zombie apocalypse team ever." *Don't ramble.*

"Do we plan to sing and draw the zombies to death?" Adrienne asked.

"Dustin can swim. Zombies typically can't. They'd get all waterlogged."

"Eww." Adrienne's grimace was priceless. "But also accurate. And depending on what kind of zombies we're talking about, they're drawn to noise. I mean, are these classic Romero zombies? World War Z? Shamblers, runners, self-aware, just drones?"

"You know your zombies." I was impressed, but I shouldn't be surprised. She knew her aliens, too.

"That's what I'm bringing to the party. But we can't offer people up as bait."

"Definitely not." Especially not with the nagging behind my ribs at the thought of losing any of them —especially Adrienne or Dustin. I was taking this game *way* too seriously. "But we're creative, smart, and have an extensive knowledge of zombies, which puts us ahead of ninety-nine percent of everyone who was ever in a zombie movie or TV show."

"Right?" Adrienne shook her head with a short laugh. "Like, not a single person on TV has ever seen a zombie movie? Hard to believe."

I smiled at her amusement. This was easy. Light and fun despite the whispers in the back of my mind that wanted me to give them attention.

"But you really don't want to answer the question, do you?" Adrienne said. "That's five people, but your item was a way to get a hold of us."

Touché. "Stickler for the rules?"

"Sometimes. But mostly I'm curious. What are your four other things?"

Now that I'd moved past the hiccup of my initial answer, I could be more lighthearted about this. "Crowbar-slash-tire iron."

"Multi-purpose. Smart."

"Twinkies."

"Not so smart. You'd go out of your way to stop at a store and grab a box of Twinkies?"

I'd let her have the flavored whipped cream. But

the question was slightly different than the one we asked her. "It's a bribe in case we run into any loud-mouthed guys who *really* want a Twinkie. Besides, I have a box in the cupboard. I love Twinkies."

She wrinkled her nose and managed a look of pure disgust. "If *you* eat them, they cease to be a bribe, but really, why would you? Is it the goopy cream filling or the generically bland sponge made of corn syrup and questionable solids that does it for you?"

"Like you have a problem with cream filling," I teased.

"Not even for a second. My problem is with Twinkies."

I sighed and fluttered the back of my hand to my forehead, pretending to be faint. "Who even are you? You can't be in our camp if you don't like Twinkies."

"You're sure? One less person to share with." She made a good point.

"Okay, fine. You can stay in our group if I can grab the Twinkies. Four and five—chlorine tablets and my biggest bottle of cologne."

"I get the tablets, why the other?"

"Assuming these are Walking Dead Season One zombies, create a false trail to throw them off scent-wise. A drop or two of that stuff goes a long way."

"You let me have my whims in the sex toy shop, so I'll let you have yours."

"Much obliged." I gave her a seated half-bow.

Silence settled in to replace the silliness, and it felt right. Like there was nothing more natural than what we were doing.

"You didn't say photos." Adrienne's voice was soft.

The words shattered my calm regardless. "Of what?"

"Your family."

I didn't know how to respond or recover from the gut punch that came with the memory. "Do you blame yourself for what happened with Sean?" I kept my voice kind. I wasn't accusing her of anything, but I already knew her answer.

"Every day."

"Even though it's not your fault."

"If it wasn't my fault, I wouldn't blame myself."

It was like she crawled into my head and extracted my answers, despite the different situations and the logical voice that said *no, really, it's not my fault.* "It's not, though."

"Do you believe that?" she asked.

And I wasn't the only one who saw the parallels. My counter rose to my lips too easily. "I was in the same accident they were. It doesn't matter how long it's been, I still feel guilty that I survived and they didn't. Not only survived, but—"

"If you're going to say *walked away mostly unscarred, obviously* you didn't."

"I wasn't. But close enough." I was going to say *went on to thrive and keep living.*

"What happened?"

"Drunk driver ran a red light and struck the passenger side." How was the pain so fresh after all this time? No, *fresh* wasn't the right word. It was more like a bruise that had never gone away, but was obvious now that I was fucking with it.

She covered my hand with hers, where it sat on the concrete between us. "It's not your fault," she said. "He decided to drink that night."

"And Sean decided being a manipulative and abusive douche was more important than appreciating the amazing person you are."

"It's not the same."

It wasn't, but it was. Why was it so easy to tell her she was right, when I couldn't believe that about myself? "The mistake I made was being on the road that night, but I trusted that everyone else would follow the same rules I was. The *mistake* you made was being good and kind and genuine, and assuming everyone else would do the same." My own words hit me hard. If I couldn't blame her for wanting to see the good in people, how could I blame myself for someone else's decision?

I didn't know, but that didn't make the gnawing ghost of guilt go away.

"I'll accept it when you do," Adrienne's voice was so soft I barely heard it.

And now the silence was back. It wasn't uncomfortable, but it was heavy. Sad.

Adrienne kicked her feet in the water enough to make small splashes. "Is swimming pool sex real? And before you wonder or ask, yes, I want to talk about something else."

The question caught me off-guard and the qualifier jabbed a hole in my blanket of grief. Thank God for the distraction. "As in, do some people do it?"

"Outside of porn."

"Definitely," I said. "But the thing no one ever talks about is that chlorinated water makes an even worse lubricant than spit."

She looked at me with feigned surprise. "You can't just spit on your hand and lube up your cock?"

An ache still lived in my chest, but this made it easier to smile and ignore the pain. "You can, or rather, I can, but that doesn't mean I should."

"That's disappointing." Adrienne jutted out her bottom lip. "So much for my wicked fantasies of swimming pool sex."

"I didn't say it can't work."

"You implied it. Are you really going to let us mask this moment with sex?" she asked.

Yes. We both knew what we were doing. Yes. I jumped in the water fully clothed, and sucked in a sharp breath at the shock. It was barely cooler than the ambient air, and I recovered in seconds.

"What are you doing?" Adrienne's laugh lit up her eyes.

I grabbed her hand and tugged. "Seems like another lesson is in order."

She didn't resist when I pulled her in, and her squeal when she hit the water was intoxicating. Pressing closer, I pinned her to the edge of the pool, knotted my fingers in her hair, and held her captive while I captured her mouth. She tasted like chlorine and sugar and salvation.

The water made our clothes flow where they weren't trapped and rough where the fabric was trapped between us. Each shift of her body against mine built delicious friction, but I wanted to feel her skin.

Adrienne tugged at my shirt, and I helped her yank it off and toss it on the concrete. She trailed her fingers over my body, heat flowing between us.

I pressed my mouth to her shoulder. Her neck. The tender spot behind her ear. "Your turn." I pulled up her shirt, stealing a kiss while she was captured and loving the sound of her laughter.

Her bra followed as well, her smile never fading. Pressing against her now was much more fun, as her curves molded to my body, and the water between us vanished.

"I can see how this isn't the easiest thing," Adrienne said between giggles and sighs.

"Do you want to give up?" I hated to even

suggest it, but I also wasn't worried about her response.

Her smile turned devilish. "I like a challenge, and we're wet now, so getting out of the pool isn't going to make it any easier to take clothes off."

"I do like the way you think." And talk. And laugh. And move. And— rather than get sucked into a spiral, I fumbled with the button and zipper on her jeans. Not the easiest thing when the fabric was swollen with water, but we figured it out.

After a bit more struggling—sliding wet denim down legs was not an easy task—we discarded the rest of our clothes by the side of the pool. Her naked body against mine, water lapping around us, was an incredible sensation. The water was just cool enough to contrast the scorching heat flowing between us.

I traced my fingers along her skin, marveling at the softness, and she teased me with tentative touches. She drew her nails lightly up my arms, and I shuddered with need. Each move she made was the same combination of curious, bold, and hesitant that I'd come to expect and adore in her.

When she reached between us and gripped my cock, I didn't try to hide my groan. She shifted her weight to press her pussy against my thigh, and ground against me as she stroked.

I pulled away enough to move my fingers between her legs, and stroke along her slit. The water made for a rougher touch, but she didn't hesitate to push into me. Her core was still slick—fuck she got wet when she was turned on—and I slipped my fingers inside her.

As I pumped, she stroked me, and her hips swayed to the same rhythm. Her breathing grew more shallow, and her expression slid toward *lost in pleasure*. I loved watching her when she was turned on.

I moved back up to tease her clit, flicking and rubbing as best I could in this environment.

She moved her hands to my arms, fingers digging into muscle as her entire body tensed under me. Her cries when she came were delicious.

"I need to fuck you, but not in the water," I murmured against her skin.

She nodded, eyes half closed, lips parted, and chest heaving. I helped her out of the water, paused long enough to grab a condom from my now-soaked wallet, and guided her toward the large, circular lounge that was set back from the pool.

Adrienne lay back on the soft microfiber covered cushions, her face flushed and her mouth lifted in a smile. I couldn't help kissing again and again.

I teased along her body, up the inside of her thighs, along her stomach, and finally along her pussy, partly to make sure her juices were flowing and she was slick, but mostly because I liked playing with her.

I knelt between her legs, hands behind her knees to push, and thrust. As I slid inside her, a long, almost feral growl tore from my throat. *Fuck* she felt incredible. I knew exactly why Dustin liked fucking her—not just her tight cunt, but everything about her.

There was no restraint left to hold back, and I slammed against her hard and fast. Pounding. Squeezing her legs to keep my grip. Watching her face shift through a rainbow of expressions.

She clenched around me when she came again, pushing me over the edge. I thrust harder, faster, frantically as orgasm flowed from me, not stopping until I passed *spent*.

I dropped her legs and leaned in to rest my cheek against her chest. Her heart hammered against my ear. I wasn't sure how long we sat like that, but it was enough that my cock softened and slipped out of her.

When she shivered with a gust, I was motivated to move. "Don't go anywhere," I said against her mouth.

"Not even considering it."

I disposed of the condom, grabbed a large terry cloth blanket from the pool house, and returned to the lounge. I wrapped both of us up, holding her close and relishing the feeling of her bare body pressed into me.

A nagging tugged at my heart. It didn't matter how much fun I had, the sadness always came back.

But when I was wrapped up with Adrienne— with Dustin—it was easier to keep it at bay.

Guilt surged in, and I didn't know if I wanted to forgive myself or indulge the feeling, one felt excessive and the other seemed wrong.

27 /
dustin

Spending the weekend with my nieces was a nicer break from my regular life than I remembered. There was something about fitting my whims around someone else's schedules and needs that felt right. Was that weird?

I was in early on Monday, working in the vacant Director's office, making calls to vendors on the East Coast. I didn't expect there to be much noise this time of day, but I could easily close the door if I needed quiet. When players saw in coming days what I was planning—community giveaways around go-live—new fans would become lifetime ones.

When Phillip and Addie walked into the Art room, their voices low and heads bent together, my good mood evaporated and the reason last week ended on a down note rushed back.

Addie poked her head into the office. "Morning." Her smile was tentative but warm.

"Hey." I wasn't upset at her, even if she was still friendly with him. "You have a good weekend?"

She glanced over her shoulder at Phillip, bottom lip caught between her teeth, then back at me. "It ended a lot better than it started. You?"

"It was all right." I couldn't ignore the surge of jealousy carried on an assumption. "You guys run into each other in the parking lot?"

Pink flooded her cheeks. "I had Sean problems, so I stayed with Phillip this weekend."

"Are you all right?" I let concern temper the darker churning.

"I'm good." Her expression, mannerisms, and growing blush all said she was more than good.

I couldn't find my smile again. "I'm glad. I have to make some calls. Get the door on your way out?" The words came out more tersely than I expected.

The creases that appeared in Addie's forehead said she noticed. "Yeah. Of course."

And now I felt like a dickhead.

She turned to leave, but paused in the doorway. "I'm sorry." Her voice was hard.

"For what?"

"I don't know. Whatever you think I did. I'm not taking sides, or… I don't know."

"I don't think anything." I managed to soften my tone. "It's not your fault."

She looked at me, lips pursed and creases in her

forehead. "You're right, it's not." She walked out of the room, shutting the door behind her hard enough to rattle my coffee cup.

Getting back into the groove of work wasn't easy, but it was necessary. I poured myself into meetings, planning, and making sure people in forums were behaving themselves. But every time I hit a pause point, my gaze drifted to the office door or to my messenger. I didn't like being on the outs with Phillip and I hated that I might have hurt Addie. He was a traitor and it was his own fault, but she didn't deserve to be stuck between us.

Every time I managed to logic myself to that point, I remembered how they looked walking in together this morning, and jealousy surged back.

An email came in from Judith, with the subject line *Funding News*. That was worth dropping everything to read.

The opening few paragraphs were her standard intro—she believed in full transparency, and everyone here was an equal partner in this business.

Any other company and I would've rolled my eyes at the boilerplate language, but she meant it.

The message continued with, *After a tremendous limited public beta, I've closed a deal with a new investment partner. This means we'll be expanding sooner than antici-pated. We'll start with adding additional staff to Art and QA, but everyone can expect their team to grow.*

This is happening thanks to all of you, but special

thanks to Dustin Lane, for his extra hours and hard work keeping us looking shiny in the public eye.

We're on our way, people. This is happening.

I was grinning when I finished reading the message. Which made me happier, the praise or that we were growing? It was a tough call, but the growth won out. I wouldn't have done the work otherwise.

Way to go and *Congrats* notes trickled into my inbox and messenger.

New people meant we were going to need an official boss sooner, rather than later. Time to remind Judith, again, that I was the perfect choice for Director of Art.

And we'd be doing this without Phillip.

The reminder swung in fast and threw me off-kilter.

There was a knock and I called, "yeah."

Addie stepped into the room again, her tentative smile back. "Great news, right? And great job. But I knew that."

Thanks. That was all I needed to say. Probably give her a genuine smile as well. "If he asked you to leave with him, would you?"

Idiot.

Addie stared back, expression blank. "Excuse me?"

"Nothing. Forget it. Thank you."

"No." An edge slid into her voice. "We're not

going to forget it or pretend you didn't say it. We're not going to shrug this entire thing off. I'm not doing this again. Not for anyone, no matter how much I like you."

I— She liked me. The words were simple, but they tugged at my heart. I should be focusing on her other words instead. "Doing what?"

She crossed her arms, and the wall she'd just put up was practically tangible. "You're not the only one sitting at your desk stewing. I'm not a hole for you to stick your dick in. I'm not a doll you don't want until someone else plays with me."

Whoa, what?

"I'm okay with the fact that we haven't labeled our relationship," she said. "But you don't get to be pissy at me for violating some invisible set of rules around *me* that exist only in your head. You will *not* treat me the way Sean did."

Oh, shit. "I wasn't— No. Addie."

"It's Adrienne." Her scowl deepened. "I don't know if you're not ready to think about the consequences or if you really do just want what you can't have, but it doesn't matter. No one gets to treat me this way."

"You're right, and I wasn't—"

Addie held up a hand, silencing me. "But you were." She turned away. "I'm going to lunch," she said loudly enough for her voice to carry through both rooms.

How wrong was it that I was smug she left without more than a glance at Phillip?

I swore I could hear seconds ticking away, though there was nothing around to make that sound. The Jeopardy music was definitely in my head. I couldn't let the conversation end this way. I caught up with her at the elevator banks, just as the doors closed, hiding her scowling face.

Fuck. It was only a couple stories to the main floor, and I sprinted down the stairs, pulling a stop as the elevator opened and Addie stepped off.

"Nope." She popped on the *p*. "I said what I wanted to."

"Then let me talk." I fell into step beside her as she left the building.

She jammed her hands into her pockets and shrugged. "Free country."

"You don't owe me anything, it's true. Especially not an explanation or an apology. I'm the one who's sorry for reacting the way I did. I didn't have a right." *Good. Leave it at that.* "But Phillip's a fucking traitor." *Bad.*

We reached the light at the intersection and waited for it to change, so we could cross. The way Addie clenched her jaw wasn't encouraging. "Your problem with him isn't mine. I get why you're upset, but he was there for me this weekend."

"I—"

"Would've been too, I know." She stepped off

the curb to the coo-coo sounds of the *Walk* sign. "I'm glad your nieces had you there to take care of them. You don't get to dictate my friends because you have a problem with them."

How did she not see...? What could I say to make her understand? Would I be reacting differently if he and I didn't have the relationship we did? Friends. But more. For a while now. Did he have that with Addie, too?

I struggled for a comeback as we walked into Loading Java. I'd flitted from place to place most of my life. Getting tied down was oppressive. At work. In relationships. Even my college major. When I got to Rinslet, when I had the chance to come here, the impulse to *move on* evaporated. I'd found a place I belonged.

All thoughts I'd had before, but they hit me hard now. I was a nomad for so long, that I never really admitted I wasn't anymore.

"This place—AcesPlayed—the people we work with, they're as much family as Daria and the girls," I spoke aloud as the reality sank heavily into my bones.

Addie finally looked up at me, scowl gone, but blankness in its place.

"Phillip. You..." Only a few weeks and she was as much at the hub of things as he was. "How come he can't see it? If he's not content here, that's fine, though I don't understand. But he didn't say anything. He hid it. And you don't have a problem with that."

"Are you in line?" someone asked.

"Go ahead." I moved toward a wall that took us out of the flow of foot traffic, and Addie followed.

She fiddled with her fingers. "I can't tell you what he was thinking. This place—Aces—doesn't mean that to me. *Yet*. I see why it does for you. For Luna. Phillip made a mistake. When he figures out what it was, let him apologize."

"He doesn't know yet?"

"Do you?" she countered.

What his mistake was or mine? I searched her face. She was open, brilliant, and stunning. This amazing mystical creature who just walked into my life one day and made herself at home, as if she'd always belonged here.

"Yes," I said even as my brain tried to keep up with my mouth. "You're right. I don't get to tell you how to feel about him, despite how I feel." I settled a hand on the back of her neck. "And besides *really good together* I don't know what you and I are. But I'd like to find out." I brushed my lips over hers.

She murmured *me too* against my mouth, and kissed me back.

My pulse screamed in response, and I crushed into her harder, needing to feel *everything* about this moment. I didn't care who saw, especially when she whimpered. I dragged my mouth up her jaw to her ear. "I want to push you into the bathroom right now and see if I can make you come as loudly as you did the other night."

Addie's light laugh was intoxicating, and her palm on my chest was a tease rather than a deterrent. "No," she said softly. "You've got to earn that."

Desire and her playful tone tempered my disappointment. "How? Flowers? Suction cup dildos? Bottle caps?"

"We'll see." She nudged me back another step. "I want to say *nothing money can buy*, but you can start with lunch."

"That's fair." I grasped her hand and tugged her back into line. It didn't matter that a few people were whispering and others looked disgusted with the public display of affection. They were just jealous. "Can I still call you Addie?"

"I guess." Her sigh was exaggerated and her smile destroyed the illusion. "But only you. And the girls."

I grinned. "I make no promises for anyone else, but excellent."

We ordered food and grabbed a table.

My phone buzzed with a text from Judith. *Re: Mr. Toph. If you have ideas, I need them today.*

Shit. I still needed to deal with Nolan.

"What's wrong?" Addie asked.

I didn't want to burden her with this, she'd seemed so stressed about the issue when she first heard about it, but I was out of ideas. "Nolan is telling Judith he wants a job. He says it's only fair since we *stole his designs*."

A low growl rolled from her throat. "Arrogant fucking asshole."

"Seriously." I couldn't have said it better myself.

"Tell her you'll take the interview, but only if you get to be the one who conducts it."

I stared at her in disbelief. "What? Why? We're not going to offer him the job. The point is to figure out how to make him go away."

"How good is he?" Addie asked.

"Eh? He's not bad. Most of his work is painting on existing assets and renders." But so was a lot of what we did.

"I had to prove myself in my interview, didn't you?"

It had been a while, but yes. "Which he can do."

"But... can he?" She pulled a pen from her purse, grabbed a napkin off the table, and slid both to me. "Draw the fighter from our promo graphics."

Easy peasy. I could recreate him in my sleep. I sketched a rough outline, careful not to tear the thin paper, and handed the draft back to Addie.

"At least sign it," she said.

I scrawled my name at the bottom. "Why?"

She tucked the sketch carefully into her wallet. "Limited edition art. And it's mine."

"Don't let me find it on eBay."

She gasped. "It's *mine*. Now, what are the odds he could do the same?"

"You're brilliant." I texted Judith back with a simple note *set up the interview. I've got this*. "You're going to talk to him with me, right?"

"Why?" Addie asked.

Mostly so I didn't punch him in the smug face. "Moral support. And so I don't punch him in the smug face."

She nodded. "I'll sit in with you."

Because with the two of us together, we could do almost anything. With Phillip, we'd be unstoppable.

The thought came out of nowhere and gave me more hope than his name deserved to carry.

What if I told him I wanted him to stay? Not at work, not if he wasn't fulfilled here, but in my life?

What if I asked Adrienne to do the same. *Be my girlfriend* sounded both simplistic and completely amazing.

I was tired of not having roots, and I saw them in this company. But more, I saw them in Addie and Phillip. I needed to think this through, not because I was uncertain, but because I needed to get it right.

I tugged Addie's fingers to draw her attention. "The girls are going home in a few nights. Have dinner with me Wednesday?"

Her smile was worth more than the world. "Of course."

Now to plan the perfect next step. And decide if I could forgive Phillip enough to see if he wanted to be part of it.

28 /
adrienne

Despite my resolve to not let Sean push me out of my house, I didn't want to go home after work. Just thinking about being alone in my apartment twisted my gut into knots. I didn't know how to get past this feeling—I'd find a solution, and probably a new apartment, but I didn't have that today.

Phillip said I could stay with him as long as I needed, but despite what I told Dustin, I wasn't stubborn enough to stay caught between them. Though, Dustin came out of the office and worked in the same room as us that afternoon —promising.

When Graham called and told me Cole had a rental that had opened up, and I could stay there for a little while, I didn't ask any questions before saying *yes please.*

I felt bad that everyone was going out of their

way for me, because of this one thing, but I wasn't going to turn down the help.

Cole dropped the keys off a short while later. When work was over, Phillip drove me to my place, hung out while I packed enough to stay somewhere else for a while, and walked me to my car.

"I'm still around if you need anything," he said.

I nodded. "I'll keep that in mind, thank you."

"See you at work tomorrow. I'll wait until you're gone, to make sure you're safe."

I nodded again. Adrienne the bobblehead, that was me. A strong pull wanted a goodbye kiss, or at least a hand squeeze, but we didn't have that kind of relationship. So I climbed into my car, and drove away, leaving Phillip in my rearview mirror.

The new place was near the University, in the foothills. Traffic was a little heavy, since everyone was going home for the day, but not so much that it kept me from going a decent speed.

Despite being displaced, life was pretty good. Me from a year ago would be looking at me now and wondering how someone who fucked up so badly—who made so many mistakes, not seeing what my marriage was—deserved what I had.

A job that was challenging but fantastic. I only saw things getting better.

Two gorgeous, intelligent men who wanted me. How was that even a thing? Especially since I was greedy enough to want them both. They'd need to

247

get real cool with each other real fast though; I hated that Phillip and Dustin were fighting. I wanted them to make things right with each other. I also wanted to figure out better what I meant to them, but I wasn't unhappy with the current conversations.

I took the messiest interstate loop ever to get from the freeway to Foothill Drive, and headed toward the address Graham gave me. There was a grocery store along the way, and I pulled into the parking lot. The fact that it was underground made me a little claustrophobic, but being surrounded by the after-work crowd made me feel safe. Paranoid—Sean wouldn't know I decided to stop at this one store, in the entire valley, nowhere near my work or home or friends.

I made my way through the store, grabbing enough essentials for the next few days, especially coffee and milk. I threw a box of Twinkies in the cart, too. Just because.

Maybe I could invite the guys over later this week, after Harmony and Alana were back with their mom. See if I could get them to make up, make them dinner to thank them for everything. See where the night took us—how they took me. And I was looking forward to dinner with Dustin. Was it a date? It felt like a date.

I paid for everything and headed to the parking lot. As I drew within visual range of my car, I saw a familiar shape near the vehicle. My heart paused for a moment. It wasn't Sean. It couldn't be.

It was. He hadn't seen me yet. I could go inside. Call someone.

No. I'd been direct with Dustin and Phillip, telling them they couldn't treat me that way, and they hadn't even been on the same continent as Sean. He couldn't control me through fear.

Still, when he turned, his gaze meeting mine, and he smiled, my stomach threatened to empty itself. I swallowed the nausea, forced my back straight, and pasted on a mask.

"Adrienne." He stepped in my path when I was close enough. "I was hoping to catch you without your dick of the week hanging around."

"Move. I'm done with your shit." My voice didn't shake at all, and I had no idea how I pulled that off. How did we get here? A few weeks ago, he was my annoying ex, and now there was no better term for him than *stalker*.

He didn't move.

Fine. I stepped around him, opened the trunk of my car, and put away the groceries. It killed me to keep my back to him, to not know if he'd left and not hear him speak. Voices and tires on pavement echoed strangely down here, and it was disorienting.

I finished putting my groceries away, closed the trunk, and turned. Sean stood *right there*, pinning me in place and sending my heart into my shoes. He wouldn't see my fear. I wasn't backing down.

"Back the fuck up," I said as firmly as I could, "I'm sick of your bullshit, and I'm not doing this anymore."

"God damn it, Adrienne." His voice was a low growl. He slammed his hand into my trunk. The clang reverberated around us, ringing in my ears and amplifying the hammering of my pulse in my ears.

I shrank away in fear; I couldn't help it.

"I'm sorry." His voice softened and he took a step back. "You just... Sometimes you're so very unreasonable."

"Are you all right?" A man stopped next to us, eyeing us both.

"No." I needed to say more. The words froze in my throat.

"Yes." Sean gave him a warm smile. "Couple's disagreement, you know how it goes. How old is your baby?"

A bag of diapers sat on the bottom of the cart.

The man smiled softly. "Six months. Total angel."

"I bet." Sean had flipped a switch inside, and adopted *angelic* himself.

I was wrong to want to confront him myself. "Please help me. Call the police. Something," I said.

Sean laughed and waved a hand dismissively in

my direction. "She's such a drama queen. You forget to pick up milk one time, and the world is ending, am I right?"

I knew this Sean. This was the man who convinced me for years that everything was my fault. Who made it so easy to doubt myself and the people around me.

The stranger laughed along with him, then looked at me. "Cut him a break. He's trying."

The stranger moved on, and so did everyone else who had slowed to watch the spectacle.

Fuck.

I rebuilt my courage from shattered fragments and clung to the pieces until I thought they might cut into my soul. "Leave me alone." I was firm, despite how badly my hands shook. "I'm leaving, and you're letting me. You're not following me. Walk away now or I'll scream."

"All right, Love. Don't get excited. I just wanted to work things out." He held his hands up, as if surrendering, and stepped back. "I'll give you some time to cool down."

It was too easy—there was no way this was over. I climbed into my car, my hands shaking so badly I dropped the keys twice before fitting them into the ignition. I expected to look up and see Sean standing next to my window when I finally got the car started, but he was nowhere to be seen.

New apartment would wait. Graham's house

was closest, and I was going straight there. I navigated the underground lot, and hit the sharp slope leading up to the street. As I waited for an opening in traffic so I could turn, I checked my rear view mirror.

Sean was in the car immediately behind me.

Bile rose in my throat and I couldn't swallow it down.

The street was too busy. I couldn't put any distance between us, especially with him riding my ass as cars inched forward.

The freeway was only a couple miles away. That would give me more room to maneuver, and maybe put a few cars between us if I did a little aggressive driving. As we drew closer to the on-ramp, I found an opening in the cars, and stomped on the gas to grab the spot.

Sean must have had a similar idea, because suddenly his car was beside mine, amid the blare of horns and screeching tires. I glanced sideways at him, then back at the road. There was a lot of mountain here, and a distinct absence of guard rails. I hit the on-ramp faster than I should for the sharp turn. Despite the one-lane road, he was still there.

His car flew sideways into mine, jarring me with the screech of metal and tearing the steering wheel from my hands.

I struggled to regain control, but two of my tires had already left pavement and hit dirt.

He jerked into my car again, and my stomach and heart left my body as my car tumbled down the slope.

29 /
phillip

Maybe I should've followed Adrienne back to her new place, made sure she was settled.

Maybe I should call Dustin, see if he needed any help babysitting.

What the hell was wrong with me?

My phone rang, and I answered before it finished the first tone. "Yeah."

"Hey." It was Cole. "Adrienne's been in an accident. I don't know more. She's at St. Mark's."

Not again.

I barely registered hanging up on him, grabbed my keys, and was in my car before the rest of my brain caught up with the gaping hole in my chest. I didn't know why Cole called me. I didn't care. This couldn't be happening again. Not to her. She couldn't—

I cut the thought off as I pulled into the dwindling remnants of rush hour traffic. There were still too many cars. Too many stop lights between my house and the hospital. Every pause gave me longer to dwell on horror scenarios.

If Sean was behind this, and he wasn't already in worse shape, he would be when I found him. Fresh fear salted old scars. I couldn't lose someone again. I couldn't lose *Adrienne*. She didn't even know how I felt. Hell, I barely knew how I felt, beyond that I couldn't lose her.

As I drove, I sent a voice-to-text to Dustin, repeating Cole's phone call. He deserved to know as much as I did. He'd want to know.

Fuck. *Please let her be all right.*

When I arrived at the hospital, I couldn't get inside fast enough. I headed for the man standing near the doors that led to exam rooms. Though I'd never met him, I'd recognize him even if I hadn't seen the pictures of him with Luna and Cole—his face was so much like Adrienne's. "Graham."

He looked up, stress lining his face. "Phillip?"

"Where is she? Is she all right?"

He nodded. "She's answering questions for the police while the doctors finish looking at x-rays and deciding if they need other tests."

Police. The notion added to my nausea. Sean was involved—I was almost certain of it. Why did I let her leave alone? But if she was answering questions, she was conscious and well enough to do so. I sank into the closest chair and dropped my head into my hands, exhaling noisily. What was most important for me to know? "What happened?"

"Car accident. I don't have more details on that. Cole called you because you've been looking out for her."

But not intently enough. I tried to calm myself with the knowledge that Adrienne would be all right. That she *was* all right. At the sound of the doors sliding open, my head whipped in that direction instinctively. Dustin walked in with his nieces.

He frowned when he met my gaze, but the scowl he'd worn since Friday, anytime I was around, wasn't there. He joined us, and I introduced him to Graham and regurgitated the same information I had.

"So we wait," Dustin said.

Graham shrugged. "Nothing else to do for it."

I watched Dustin with Harmony and Alana, and the void inside me grew. The girls were talking quietly and playing some sort of game on their tablets. He didn't interact with them much, but did answer the occasional question. He was so good with them. He'd be good with his own kids.

I was an idiot, surrendering a wonderful thing because of fear. Knowing I could've lost Adrienne tonight, that I was willing to push away Dustin to avoid feeling… What the fuck was wrong with me?

"I'm sorry." I spoke softly, not wanting to disturb the rest of the room.

Dustin looked up, brows raised.

"I'm sorry for keeping things from you," I said.

His mouth twisted with his frown. "You're still leaving, though."

Was I? There was no reason to change that aspect of my plan. "This doesn't mean the same thing to me. But I'm still sorry for the secret."

Dustin nodded, and turned his attention to Harmony when she tugged his sleeve. "You're supposed to forgive people when they're sorry," she whispered.

Dustin sighed. "Alana, watch your sister. I'm just going to be over there, but keep an eye on her."

"Okay." Alana pointed at Harmony's screen and murmured something.

Dustin jerked his head toward a pair of vending machines, and I followed him. He leaned against a nearby wall, arms crossed over his chest and attention on his nieces. "You don't have to go. We're hiring new people."

I have to. The retort lodged in my throat. I didn't have to—my reason for leaving was diminished and Adrienne proved there was still work for me at Aces-Played. But she was both a different case and part of the reason I couldn't completely abandon the idea of walking away.

She was okay. Graham looked pretty sure of that. But even the brief time where I thought I'd lost her... The feeling hadn't hit me so hard with Dustin yet because I could still see him. Even mad at me, he didn't feel gone.

"We don't have to lose touch, even if I leave," I said.

"*Lose touch*," Dustin scoffed. "You still don't... It's okay, I didn't get it either."

"It?"

He scrubbed his face. "It feels weird to have this conversation now, but a text like the one you sent me, the fact that we're here, drives home that sometimes there's not a tomorrow. We're lucky this time there is."

I knew that all too well.

"I'm still pissed that you lied to me," Dustin said. "But I don't want you gone from my life. Aces-Played, this game, is something I've searched for my entire life and didn't know it until I found it. And so are you."

Words lodged in my throat. I needed air. I turned away and Dustin grabbed my arm. "You don't get to do that tonight," he said. "You're going to hear me out."

"I'm listening."

"I'm tired of calling what you and I have *friend-*

ship. I didn't realize it before, and it's as much my fault that it took so long as anyone's. You and I... we're more."

The words should hurt to hear, but they sounded so good. Something was missing, though. "What about Adrienne?" He was so good with her. I was so happy with her. And with him. "You dropped everything for her."

"So did you," Dustin said. "She needs us. I need you. Here, with us. Yes, us. I want her too, but I have to start somewhere. I'm not going to miss the chance. And the instant she's out here, I'm going to tell her something similar. Except, I've never said this before. Not in this context."

I knew what was coming, even if I couldn't articulate it, and it both terrified me and filled me with anticipation.

"Alana will be so heartbroken." Dustin let out a shaky laugh. "I love you. I'd be devastated if I lost you."

"I love you too." I didn't know which felt better, hearing the words or saying them. A huge weight lifted from my chest, and I felt like I could breathe, could think, more clearly than in ages.

I leaned in to brush my lips over his, the soft kiss hurting and healing at the same time. He pressed his mouth to mine, lingering before pulling away with a soft smile.

"Talk more later?" I asked.

"I'm holding you to that."

I brushed a thumb over Dustin's bottom lip, and moved so he could rejoin his nieces. I moved to face the room, and stayed where I was, watching the room. Watching Dustin as he went back to exchanging whispers with Alana and Harmony. I was an idiot. How did I ignore this for so long?

Was he right? Could I stay at AcesPlayed? Maybe we could create some sort of training position. I did that anyway, but it would be nice to make it official.

I'd worry about that later. For now, I needed to see Adrienne, get that confirmation she was okay and find out what happened. My thumbs hooked in my pockets, I drummed my fingers on my leg and tried not to stare too long at the clock on the far wall.

When the doors finally opened, and a nurse rolled Adrienne out in a wheelchair, I wanted to sprint across the room and pull Adrienne into a tight hug followed by a long kiss.

Given the bruises marring her face and the fact her arm was in a sling, I'd probably have to be more gentle than that. A glance at Dustin, and the ambivalence splayed on his face, he was probably dealing with similar thoughts.

The nurse looked at Graham. "You're the brother?"

He nodded and joined them. He squeezed Adrienne's good hand. "You're all right?"

"Dislocated shoulder. Lots of bruises. A bit of mental trauma, but I'll live," Adrienne's smile was weak and her voice tired.

Harmony ran up to Adrienne and stopped short. "Can I give you a hug? Does it hurt? I have Hello Kitty bandaids in my backpack. Do you need one?"

"I have enough bandaids for now, but I might need some later. You can hold my hand." Adrienne reached out.

Harmony grasped her hand tightly.

"Your girl?" The nurse asked.

Adrienne shook her head and opened her mouth.

"Nieces," Alana said.

I met Dustin's gaze, and his raised eyebrows reflected mine. She was either pretending she didn't see us kiss, or was far more understanding of the concept *you can love more than one person* than most adults. Either way, she was probably going to take over the world when she was old enough. Or next year.

"Well, I'll let you tell them what happened and catch up." The nurse patted Adrienne lightly on her good shoulder. "She's got her prescriptions and our contact information. Call us or bring her back here if there are any complications, but she should be fine. Stay safe, hon."

"Thank you." Exhaustion radiated from Adrienne.

My impulse to take her away from all of this surged even stronger. I settled for asking, "What happened?"

Her laugh was strained. "For as many ways as I've told the police, I should ask them to give you a copy of their report."

Dustin gently tugged Harmony away. "Go get that bandaid," he said. "So Addie has it later."

She nodded and ran to her backpack.

"Short version, Sean ran me off the road."

At Adrienne's words, I balled up my fists.

"Is he here? Can we see him?" Dustin asked before I could.

"He is, but you probably can't," Adrienne said. "He's got a police guard. And a shattered femur. As soon as he can be moved, they're extraditing him to Washington, where he has warrants for assault." She dragged in a shaky breath.

I was simultaneously sick and furious at the implication. But she was all right and out of his reach. I wanted to take her away, hide her from the world, and pamper her. Keep her safe. Tell her how much I loved her.

Harmony ran up to Adrienne, several bandaids clutched in her fist. "Here you go. These will help."

"Thank you." Adrienne took the presents and tucked them into her purse. She looked at Graham, her face taut with stress. "Can I...?"

"Luna has the guest room ready, and she can grab some of your stuff for you. You can stay with us as long as you need." Graham stepped behind her and grabbed the handles of her wheelchair. "Let's get you out to the car if you're ready."

Adrienne glanced between Dustin and me. "I don't know why you're here, but it means a lot that you are. Between the trauma and the police and the injuries and the painkillers, though... I need sleep. Catch up later?"

"Sure." I stepped close enough to squeeze her fingers. "Get some rest."

Dustin brushed his lips over her cheek. "We're here."

Graham rolled Adrienne out of the emergency room.

Dustin turned to me. "I have to put them to bed. And give them a multivitamin since I let them eat vending machine food for dinner. You'll be in the office tomorrow?"

"Yeah." And probably for a while. I wasn't one-hundred percent positive yet, but I was pretty sure I was staying with the company for a while. I gave him a quick kiss, and it felt more natural than I'd ever expected. "We'll catch up then."

What a roller coaster of a night. Now that I had

answers—resolution—adrenaline settled heavily inside. Dustin was right—about a lot of things, but one specifically—there was always a chance tomorrow wouldn't get here.

Fear wasn't going to keep me from experiencing *today* again.

30 /
adrienne

Maybe I was destined to live in guest rooms for the rest of my life.

The thought was more bleak than I wanted to feel. Or maybe I just didn't want to feel right now. Not anything. Because some of the thoughts in my head were dark and some were cruel and hope was there too, though it was so very hard to grasp and it seemed like the last thing I should be focusing on.

I sat on the bed in the guest room in Graham's house—technically I supposed it was Cole's house, but they both lived here with Luna, so that was all semantics.

And was I really having a mental conversation with myself over house ownership?

It was better than the alternative—putting words to my more insistent and pervasive thoughts.

I was propped up by and surrounded by more pillows than a Bed, Bath, & Beyond, so I could make myself comfortable however I needed. I had pain pills for my shoulder. The thought of taking those was a little terrifying, because if they blanked my mind I might like it too much and if they didn't...

I didn't want to sleep with intense, drug-induced dreams.

Luna knocked on the open door frame, and came in without waiting for an answer. She sat at the other end of the bed. "How are you doing?" She radiated concern and sympathy.

Which made a tight lump grow in my throat. "I don't know."

She pulled her legs under her and crossed them. "Okay."

I didn't like the silence that sank in, sitting heavy in my joints. Pressing against my lungs. It was like being alone, but now someone was watching me mentally fracture like a late-in-life Picasso. "You didn't bring your cards. I thought you might offer to read for me or something."

"No," Luna said plainly.

"Why not?"

"It's not what you need right now."

A bitter laugh slipped past my lips. "How do you know that? *I* don't know what I need right now."

"Just a feeling." Her tone was kind and free of judgement.

What was I supposed to say?

Silence stretched on. Why was Luna still here? Not that I minded her company, but this wasn't company—it was as confusing as everything else. What was I supposed to think? To feel? Was one of us supposed to say something?

"I'm just tired of it all." My own words caught off-guard, coming from nowhere but feeling right. "I'm tired of people who think they deserve anything their whims demand. Of people who think only they matter. Who don't stop to consider the consequences of their actions… or don't care."

I paused, surprised at my own words—not that I blurted them out without thinking, but that I was able to put any form to my feelings, even if it was a vague blob of a form. I waited for Luna to reply. To argue or add her thoughts. Anything.

She looked up, understanding in her gaze. "I get that."

"I believed all the rules when I was growing up." Apparently I wasn't done. "Sometimes I feel like I was wrong to do so. Like everyone else knew they were more like loose guidelines that could be ignored unless someone needed to be kept down."

"Which rules?" Luna asked.

"*Do unto others,*" I recited. "If you work hard, that's how you get ahead. That life rewards the industrious. That if things go wrong in your life—if you fail, if someone else does better than you, if the world beats you down and kicks you in the gut until you can't breathe and you don't know how you're going to make it to tomorrow, that it's your own fault." I drew in a deep breath, to make sure I still could. I didn't feel as bleak as that sounded, but there were times in the past where I had.

"Maybe it is my fault." The words flew out more from habit than because they tasted real. "Some things are, but not everything. I'm not perfect. I blurt out inappropriate things. I let opportunities pass me by because I'm scared. But I'm trying to. To do right by me. To not harm others along the way. And not because I *should*, but because I want to. I want the people around me to feel good, and I don't want to feel shitty either. I never want to be responsible for someone else's suffering. I don't want to miss out on experiences. I want to experience the world, and I don't mind hard work. What I mind are people who think they can grind the rest of us under the heel of their boot because in their mind no one is more important than them.

"People lie and cheat and steal and run their ex-wives off the road and assault women they've dated and think it's their right because they want to and as long as they smile at the right people and believe their own bullshit, they so frequently get away with it. And the people they hurt, the people who let it happen because they think it's their fault or because they don't see it or because they think if they're just a little nicer..."

I forced myself to stop, before I lost any more track of my own words, and focused on Luna. "Are you going to say anything?"

"I agree."

The simplicity of her reply almost made me laugh. I didn't feel good enough to laugh, though I did feel lighter than when she came in here. "Anything besides that."

She shook her head. "I think you're covering it pretty well."

"That's a longer version of *I agree*. I didn't deserve what Sean did to me. No one does. Even if someone is a total, inconsiderate narcissist, like him, that's not justice. That kind of *an eye for an eye* doesn't get anyone anywhere. But I'm still glad he's hurt. Does that make me a bad person too? I'm glad he's in traction, and not just because he won't be able to get up for a while. I'm glad he's in pain, and that for once, I'm dealing with less than he is. How horrible am I?"

"You're not at all," Luna said.

"You wouldn't be thinking things like this. How repulsive am I right now?"

"I've never wished a man dead, but I have read some obituaries with great pleasure."

A dry smile cracked my face. "Graham says that."

"Pretty sure someone else said it first, but yeah, I got it from him." Luna crawled closer, until her knees touched my feet. "I don't like seeing people in pain. I hate knowing I caused it or believe I could've prevented it. But there are times when we have to ignore that instinct, especially when it's not our fault. And this isn't your fault."

"I know that, but at the same time, sometimes it's so very hard to believe it."

"I won't tell you to stop feeling what you're feeling, or that you're wrong about any of this. There are some people who need to hear that, though I probably wouldn't tell them either, but you don't. Anyone who tells you otherwise is an idiot," Luna said. "Everything inside you—the good, the bad, and the uncertain—it's all valid. Doesn't matter what we've been taught. No one is any more allowed to dictate your thoughts than you are responsible for their actions."

What she was saying was wise, but at the same time, "You know it's not that easy."

"I do." Luna brought her leg to her chest and rested her chin on her knee. "It's a hard thing to remember, and I have to remind myself about it on a regular basis. I'll remind you too, if you want. The *rules* you mentioned, some people follow them, some don't. We can only say how we act."

"How do we know if we're acting right?"

"You are."

"But how do you *know*?" I hated this uncertainty. The assholes never looked like they had to deal with this kind of doubt. What would it be like to have that kind of faith in my own heart?

Luna grinned. "Because I'm a fucking genius and I can tell."

I wanted so badly to believe her. She was a genius. "What if I fall again, and it's a mistake again?" There was a fear I hadn't wanted to look at. But now that my head was shifting itself into order, it was easier to pick out the thoughts.

"Phillip?"

"And Dustin." When I'd seen them at the hospital, the warmth had pushed away a lot of my pain.

"They're not bad guys. If you don't believe me, Cole is a good judge of character."

My smile felt lighter this time. "Phillip said something similar. He said that was how he knew I was all right."

"Pfft. You're better than all right. You're amazing. And here's the thing, if you fall and it doesn't work out... Well, I hate to be cliché, but it's better to have loved and lost... Would you really give up the good to not have to feel the bad? If you need to, as hard as it is, take the whole Sean experience out of the equation."

Would I give up the last few weeks with Dustin and Phillip if it meant avoiding the risk? If it meant I could guarantee my heart was shielded? "No. I wouldn't give it up."

"There's your answer. Also, *nice*. I mean, you're

way out of their league, and who wants a nearly forty year old bachelor? But they're both pretty. And probably smart."

I felt better with each passing moment. My doubt wasn't gone, but it was hiding behind sunshine. Luna was at least half teasing, because her boyfriends were Phillip and Dustin's age, and she was distinctly younger than me. "They are pretty. And smart. Mostly. I'm not sure they're completely in touch with their feelings."

Luna scrunched up her nose. "Not everyone is. Graham said they looked completely panicked when they got to the hospital, so I think they're on the right track. If they're not, you'll just have to tell them so."

"I can do that."

"I know." Luna shifted to lay next to me, her head on my legs. Hugs were hard because of my arm and the bruises, but this worked fine for me. My head was as much of a mess as my body, but I could see past the jumble to the truth now. It had been a long time since I felt this clear-headed about something.

31 /
dustin

I hated not being able to act. Especially after the emotional wringer of last night. Waiting to talk to Addie. Waiting for the *interview* with Nolan... Patience was not one of my virtues. Which was why I was in the office too early, trying to occupy my mind with anything else.

But one thing was incredible about last night, and I needed more time with Phillip to explore it. Not him so much, because I'd done a lot of exploring there, but we could always revisit old favorites and map new paths. Our shared *I love yous* still sang in my thoughts. I never realized how good that could feel until now.

And as soon as I got a hold of Addie, she'd hear it too. I sent her a text earlier saying I hoped she was doing okay and I missed her. I'd wait at least a little bit before I bugged her again.

When I heard Phillip come in, I didn't look up

from my work. "Hey, traitor." It was hard to keep my voice stern.

No response.

I finally moved from behind my screen to find him staring at me, mouth twisted.

"Did I imagine last night?" he asked flatly.

I smiled. Nope. I had no patience to draw out that kind of teasing. "Not unless I did too."

Phillip rolled his eyes, but bent to give me a quick kiss before taking his seat. He paused. "Was that weird?"

"Kind of. But weird-good. I liked it."

"Me too. You talk to Adrienne yet?"

"No. I texted her."

"Me too." Phillip turned to his computer.

When I thought about what happened, I saw red. It was a shame I couldn't go *talk* to Sean now.

I would be talking to Nolan, though. Probably still not a good idea to punch him in the smug face, but the impulse was stronger now than ever. I wanted Addie here, not to temper me, but so I'd know she was ok.

We got a pair of messages from Luna and Judith, letting us know Addie wouldn't be working today. But, Luna assured us, she was doing as well as could be expected, and was just resting.

When Ivan called back to tell me my ten o'clock was here, I was out of my seat before he finished talking. I made my way to the small conference room, where Nolan was waiting. With a smile that probably showed too many teeth, I shook his hand. "It's been a while."

"It has. Good to see you." His tone was cheer-flavored bullshit.

"Sorry I'm late." At the sound of Addie's voice I whirled toward the doorway. Her arm was in its sling, and her expression was blank-leaning-toward-sad. "I'm Adrienne." She offered her hand.

Nolan shook it. "Nice to meet you." Nolan smiled warmly. "Are you all right? May I ask what happened?"

"I'm not, and you may not." Addie clipped off the words as she took the seat next to me.

I did love her. "Let's get started. I've got your resume and portfolio, but tell me a bit about what you've been doing for the last couple of years."

We ran through a list of boilerplate questions. Addie was quiet the whole time, and Nolan was flippant with his answers. But to his credit, they were real answers—he was treating this like an interview he had to do well on—I just didn't like the under-lying conviction that he already had the job.

"We do have a practical test part of our inter-view process," Addie said when we reached a pause. She grabbed the notepad from the stack I'd brought in here, and slid it across the table along with a pencil.

"That's right." I stepped in to back her up. "Our

players have high expectations. We need to make sure you bring your own style to the table, but can still operate within the parameters we've already established for the game."

"In other words, you need good copy-ers?" Nolan's question was smug. "I see why you're here."

Addie pressed her leg to mine under the table, cutting off my retort. "This is your interview, not Dustin's. Draw a picture of our orc priest. Any of the poses from our site, or your own interpretation is fine too."

I couldn't hide my smirk. That was one of the designs he claimed I'd stolen.

For the first time since I walked in the room, Nolan's smile vanished, and a scowl took its place. "This is for a *digital* art job. Where's a computer? A drawing tablet?"

Addie didn't miss a beat. "We all work with our hands as well. Concept sketches, other things. This is the interview requirement, and looking at your portfolio, it shouldn't be an issue."

She and I watched as he scribbled his way through a recreation that looked nothing like his art or mine.

"That'll be fine," I stopped him when he had a rough concept in place. It was too painful to wait for more, no matter how much I wanted to see him crash and burn.

"I'm not done," Nolan said.

This was where I'd say *we'll get back to you*, and send him on his way to let him stress and stew.

Addie slid the notepad away from him and studied it. "Your work has potential, but it's not up to our standards." No pulling punches with her today. Or most days. "If you'd like to take a few classes, I can recommend some great teachers, and you're welcome to re-apply in a year or two."

Nolan turned red. I'd never seen that literally happen to someone who was angry. "This is a bullshit test. The environment is shitty and you sat and watched me the whole time. I don't need to *prove my skill* because Dustin stole the art you already have. That *is* my skill."

Anger surged inside me.

Addie covered my hand with hers, and smiled sweetly at Nolan. "You're a liar."

"Excuse me?" Nolan stared at her in disbelief.

"You don't have the skill to do this job. If you want to steal someone else's work, this isn't the place to do it." She set the notepad back on my stack. "This will go to our attorneys. If you threaten us again, they will tie you up in court for years, and we will *not* keep things quiet. Can you really afford that hit to your wallet? Your career?"

"Are you threatening me, you stupi—"

"Get out." I had to cut him off because if he finished that sentence, I'd deck him. I was already looking for an excuse. "We're done here."

Addie's sugary sweet smile never faded. "Have a lovely day." She offered her hand.

He scowled and stormed from the room.

I followed to make sure he actually left the office, then turned to Addie, who had come with us. I didn't know what to say first. That she kicked ass in there. That I was so happy to see her. That I loved her desperately and I didn't want her going back to anyone's house but mine or Phillip's?

"Judith is in Art and wants to see both of you," Ivan said before I could pick an option.

"You were brilliant in there." I told Addie as we headed to our offices. Everything else tried to push its way out, but would have to wait.

Her saccharine smile was gone, and now the exhaustion around her eyes and mouth was obvious. "Thanks. I was a little pissed off. Did it show?"

"I wasn't even looking for that. Fuck him if he didn't like it."

"But don't." Her tone lifted and I glanced at her to see a corner of her mouth tugged up.

We walked into Art to find Judith had made herself at home at an empty desk and was chatting with Phillip. "How'd the interview go?" she asked.

"Addie handled it. The problem is gone." There were few things I was more certain of.

Judith didn't look convinced. "I've heard that before."

I patted my sketchpad. "If he comes back, it won't be an issue, I guarantee it."

"Good," Judith said.

"I get that you're all pals, but in my world, boss sitting in the office doesn't mean good things." Addie sounded apprehensive. "What's up?"

Judith gave a rare soft smile. "No beating around the bush, then. You all saw the announcement about funding, but in order for that to work, this department needs some changes."

No shit. This was it. She was here to give me my job. *Dustin Lane—Director of Art.* It had an incredible ring to it.

"I've withdrawn my resignation," Phillip said.

"*Yes.*" I didn't try to hide my excitement. "Fuck yeah. Told you that you couldn't quit us."

He clucked and shook his head. "You didn't say that specifically, but you are right."

"And Phillip's moving into the role of Director of Art." Judith's words brought my brain grinding to a halt.

What in the ever living fuck? He couldn't. I'd done everything right. I'd made this company *shine* in the public eye. If I thought I felt betrayed before—

"Before you blow a fuse." Judith cut off the thought, and I clenched my jaw. "I wanted to have this conversation with you in private, Dustin, but I also didn't want this news getting back to you before you and I spoke. I'm really impressed with the work you've done. More than your job. You've gone above and beyond. I didn't think we'd need a marketing team when we started, but we wouldn't have come this far without you. You don't have to answer me now, but I'd like you to start a new team as Director of Marketing and Community."

Wait. What? I let out a short laugh. "No. Yeah? You're serious."

She started back, expression bland. "Have you ever known me to joke?"

"There was that one time—"

"Shut it." She cut Phillip off with a glare.

He shrugged.

I wanted to hear that story.

Judith turned back to me. "Think about it. Get me your answer by Wednesday."

"There's no need. My answer is yes." Absolutely. This was better than I expected. This was... *wow*.

"Great," Judith said. "Contracts will be in your emails in the next couple of days. Office is Phillip's. Dustin, pick one of the empty rooms for you and your team. Adrienne, go home. For the rest of the week. What are you even doing here?"

"I told Dustin I'd help him with the interview." Addie's reply was firm.

"I don't care," Judith said. "And this isn't up for negotiation. How did you even get here? Tell me you're not driving."

"Cole dropped me off."

Judith rolled her eyes. "That man, I swear."

"I begged him to."

I'd never seen anyone counter Judith so completely, without sounding even a smidge aggressive. Another reason to be impressed with Addie.

"One of you take her home. *Now*." With that, Judith left.

"Do you think she actually meant *now*?" Phillip looked at us.

I shook my head. "No. I'm sure there was some room for interpretation."

"Do I get a say in this?" Addie asked. "I feel like I should be the one to say where I go and when and with whom."

"I mean, yeah, but also… if the boss says *go home* do you really argue?" That didn't make sense to me. At least not as a general concept.

Addie scrunched up her nose. "Phillip's my boss now."

"Judith's word still overrides mine," Phillip said.

This was ridiculous. We were wasting words when something far more important needed to be discussed. "I'll take you back to Graham's. If you want. But first"—I rested a gentle hand on her cheek, careful to avoid the bruises, and brushed my lips lightly over hers. I wanted to do more, but I didn't want to hurt her. "I have to tell you I love you."

Pink crept up her neck. "That's... anti-climactic."

I stared at her in disbelief, and failed to ignore she hadn't said it back. "I had a whole speech planned. Dinner Wednesday night. But I'm supposed to be taking you home *now*, so you get the abbreviated version until I have time for more."

"Except we're still here," Addie said.

"I'll give you a flowery speech." Phillip reached past us to close the office door, then stepped up next to Addie. He grasped her fingers and brought them to his lips, kissing one at a time. "I can't imagine a future without you. Last night was terrifying, not knowing if you were all right. I don't want to let you go. I will, if that's what you want, but I'll do everything in my power to prove how incredible we would be together. Anything you ask. I love you, Adrienne."

She caught her bottom lip between her teeth. "I love you too. Yesterday was hard, but seeing you at the hospital when I got out... I wish I'd felt up to sticking around, and that I hadn't already used up so many words in the last day or so. I love you."

I cleared my throat loudly, drawing their attention. "Excuse me? Phillip didn't even figure it out until I told him, and I was going to say it to you first, Addie, but then you were hurt, and now he's stolen my thunder. I love you too. I'd do anything for you too."

Addie focused on me, still gripping Phillip's hand. "But you did say this to each other?"

Did that matter at this moment? "Yes."

"*God* I was wondering how long that would take." Her exclamation caught me off-guard. Before I could reply, she rose on her toes and kissed me on the cheek, then the lips. "And I love you too. You're both stupid boys, with stupid egos. But I love you, Dustin. And as much as I love a public display of affection, one, I don't want to get fired if Judith finds out I'm still here, and two, I don't want to get fired for doing anything *inappropriate* in the office. Again." She smirked.

"Eh, we'll save that for after hours." I kissed her on the tip of the nose. "And *fine*, I'll take you home. But tomorrow night, as soon as my place is my own again, you're mine—ours."

"I'm yours now," Addie said. "But yes. Definitely."

I hated to wait, patience was not a virtue of mine, but Addie and Phillip were worth waiting for.

32 /

adrienne

Phillip treated me to another incredible and drawn-out kiss before I left the office. And after a long goodbye kiss from Dustin at home that wasn't nearly long enough, I made him go back to work. I didn't like that I had to wait until tomorrow night to see them again, but I did need to heal at least a little more.

Their words, the sweet, the sexy, and mostly the love, both helped and added to the feeling of missing them. The rush of hearing *I love you* from two different, both incredible men was better than any painkiller high. It was enough to fall asleep to, in a longer nap than I'd taken in ages.

Dinner and watching TV after with Graham, Luna, and Cole was nice—it was fun to sit and catch up and talk and poke fun at our favorite characters on the screen—but when I got a text from

Dustin, I excused myself to my temporary room, and closed the door behind me.

What are you wearing? Dustin's message read. He'd added Phillip to the thread too.

The lead-in was cute, but I wasn't feeling particularly sexy. *A sling, and the baggiest nightgown I own.*

Hot. Send pics, Phillip wrote.

I shook my head at the empty room. *I feel way too hammered for that.*

Instead of either of them replying, my phone rang. "Hello," I answered.

"You're gorgeous no matter what," Dustin greeted me.

"You happy now?" Phillip's sigh was exaggerated. "You got to the sweet line first this time?"

It felt incredible to smile. "Next contest—who's going to send me the first dick pic?"

"Dude. Inappropriate," Phillip said.

Now I was laughing. "Don't tell my boss on me."

"What's in it for me?" Dustin asked. "I'll show you *my* dick."

"Moment's passed, and I've seen it." God this felt good. Natural. It didn't matter that the conversation was ridiculous, I loved it.

Dustin snorted. "Are you kidding me right now?"

"I don't even know anymore. I'm just having fun." So much fun.

"I miss you." Phillip's tone softened. "My pillows won't smell like you much longer."

"Uuuugh." Dustin dragged the word out. "Creepy, dude."

"Jealous much?" Phillip countered.

Yup. Still grinning. "I miss you too. Both of you. And I miss my vibrators." Where did that come from? Didn't matter—I was rolling with it. "I wonder if Luna will make an extra trip..."

"You're putting us in the same category as *battery operated* boyfriends?" Dustin sounded hurt.

I had a feeling he wasn't really, but I'd reassure him anyway. "Not even for a heartbeat. But I have a feeling they'll be far gentler with me."

"Challenge accepted," Dustin said. "Tomorrow night, we'll show exactly how gentle we can be."

"Hard to be rough having dinner." I wouldn't be able to pretend even a second longer that was all I thought we were going to do.

"Depends on who we're having for dinner," Phillip said.

"You, in case that wasn't clear," Dustin added.

I assumed, but I liked the confirmation. "Promises promises."

"So many of them." It was Dustin's turn to shift to sincere. "As many promises as you want. From now until forever."

This was definitely perfect.

We talked for at least another hour, until I

started yawning and couldn't stop. "I promise, it's not you, it's me," I assured them between yawns.

"We know," Dustin teased.

Phillip made me promise to get some sleep, we all exchanged *I love yous*, and I forced myself to hang up, despite wanting to fall asleep with their voices in my ear.

My phone buzzed a few minutes later with two new texts. Phillip had sent me a picture of a Twinkie, and Dustin provided a picture of Richard Nixon.

I couldn't help my smile at the two dick pics, provided in the way only the two of them would.

The next day my bruises were a lovely shade of violet-turning-yellow. I hated it. When I got *good morning* texts from both Phillip and Dustin, I had to warn them not to be horrified when they saw me.

They assured me they didn't care, and I'd need to say *no* if I was trying to get out of tonight.

That was enough to silence me. I definitely didn't want to put off seeing them again.

The day crawled slowly, and I wasn't sure if it was because I didn't dare do much, or because I was looking forward to tonight.

No, I knew it was a mix of both, but my impatience was more about tonight. The long bath in a tub big enough to cover my boobs and knees with water at the same time was a nice break, and it was strangely comforting having Luna help me dry and style my hair.

None of that stopped me from counting the seconds until Phillip picked me up. He gave me a long kiss on the front step, and another before he opened the car door for me.

"I've never had this with anyone," I murmured against his mouth.

He pulled back and studied me. "Kisses and chivalry?"

"Not like this. Not where it feels genuine and natural rather than done like it was expected and preferred forgotten."

He kissed me again. "Their loss. And we need to go, or else I'll keep you out here for way too long, and Dustin is preparing for dinner."

This entire situation felt surreal. I remembered being there yesterday at the office, but the pain from the accident had been close enough it muted the memory. Phillip's kisses made it all feel more real, though, and I was happy to keep making new memories. As many as possible.

Phillip kept contact with me in one way or another—my hand, my thigh—most of the drive to Dustin's. When we arrived, Phillip knocked and Dustin called, "It's open."

We found him in the kitchen, putting something in the fridge, the counters empty. He gave Phillip a quick kiss, then wrapped an arm around my waist and pulled me closer for a longer one that stole my breath.

Dustin didn't let me go after, and I loved the feeling of being pressed against him. He brushed his lips over my cheek, my neck, and the edge of my ear. "*Someone* stole my thunder yesterday, and I didn't get to tell you everything I wanted to."

"I'm listening." I turned my ear—one of the non-bruised bits of me—toward him, angling for more attention.

He obliged, nipping lightly at my earlobe, his hot breath teasing my skin. "I don't care if the entire rest of the world thinks I'm a *party boy*. What you think, what Phillip thinks, is more important than anything. I want you in my future, for as far as I can see and beyond. I want stability and a family and I want those things with you."

"I want those things too." Forever and beyond was a long time, and instead of fear, I was excited at the possibility.

Phillip stepped behind me, and I was wrapped in comfort and kisses and strong, protective arms.

"I was told you were making dinner." Go me, ruining the moment.

"Technically I said he was preparing for dinner." Phillip's words rumbled through my back.

"That feels like a tiny, semantic difference."

Dustin smirked. "But it's one that makes all the difference."

I was missing something. "Then... what's for dinner?" Yesterday it was supposed to be me, but that didn't seem to be the case now.

"Not until after dessert," Phillip said.

Dustin dipped his head to brush his mouth over my ear again. "That's you—dessert—in case there was any confusion."

"Which answer gets me devoured faster?"

"That one." Phillip's reply was low and seductive.

They led me upstairs to a room whose door had been closed every other time I was here. The art that hung in thin metal frames on the walls was varied and bright, a beautiful contrast to the dark bedding and furniture.

It felt very much like Dustin.

He stopped in front of me, and Phillip moved to my back.

Dustin dragged his thumb along my bottom lip before following the same path with my mouth. "We're going to be gentle, but stop us if anything hurts too much."

"Okay." The thought of some kinds of pain was tempting, but not the twisting-my-shoulder-wrong kind.

I'd worn a loose button-down top, because it was easier for me to get in and out of. Phillip kissed along the back of my neck, while Dustin worked his way down the buttons of my shirt.

Dustin teased the fabric aside, brushing it across a bare breast. "No bra?" he asked with a smirk.

"They're a pain to put on, and I figured you'd just be taking it off…"

"I've always known you were a genius." He threw the top aside. The frown that slid across his face vanished just as quickly.

But I didn't like the look of it. "What's wrong?"

Phillip brushed his lips over my shoulder. "He probably hates seeing the bruises as much as I do."

"Not because they're ugly, but because I suspect they hurt." Dustin kissed a larger purple spot near my stomach.

"Some do, some don't." I sighed at the barely-there sensation of their mouths on my skin. "I don't think the kisses will help them heal any faster. Not that I want you to stop."

"It might help," Dustin drew his tongue lightly up the middle of my chest, along my collarbone, and pressed his mouth to mine again.

Phillip's *pft* teased my back. "He thinks his love heals everything."

"It does help with quite a few things," I said.

Dustin smirked and dragged a thumb over my nipple. "Because I'm amazing."

"You really are." I sighed at the double attention. "When you're not being dense." I couldn't help the playful jab."

"*Ha.*" Phillip sounded smug.

I rolled my eyes, though he wouldn't see. "I mean you too."

"We're trying to make up for that." Dustin lowered his head again to draw one of my nipples into his mouth, licking so gently it drove me wild.

"You're doing great so far." I managed between moans.

Between kisses and light touches, they stripped off the rest of my clothes, and guided me toward the bed. Phillip sat behind me, propping me up and teasing his fingers along my stomach and over my chest.

Dustin knelt in front of me. He started at my mouth, and dragged his lips down my body.

Anticipation built inside at the notion of where he was headed. "I'm going to get used to this if you two aren't careful."

"We're only being careful until you're healed." Phillip kneaded my breast gently.

Dustin drew his tongue along my hip. "But you deserve to be used to this, and so much more."

He nudged my legs further apart as he dropped lower on the mattress and moved his head between my legs. My pulse screamed as his hot breath teased my damp skin, and when he licked along my slit, my heart skipped a beat before picking up double-time.

Phillip rolled a nipple between his fingers, and when Dustin plunged his tongue inside me, Phillip dropped his other hand to tease my clit.

I couldn't focus on any one sensation, as much as I wanted to memorize them all. The feelings all flowed together, making my head feel light as air. My thoughts floated away and climax built inside. Nudging me. Coaxing. Drawing me closer until I tumbled into orgasm.

I let the scream of pleasure out, not caring if the world heard, digging my fingers into Phillip's wrist until it was all too much.

They eased away gently, and Dustin rose to crush his mouth to mine, letting me taste myself, devouring my moans. He moved to Phillip, and their grunts near my ear were delicious.

"Wow." I tried to grasp for something more. "I've never... Wow." A realization slipped in and I couldn't hide my faint frown.

"What's wrong?" Dustin asked.

"I'm not sure I'm up for more." Inspiration struck. "I'd love to watch the two of you together."

Dustin's huff was exaggerated. "We're not a fetish."

"You're *my* fetish," I said. "I'll beg."

"You're definitely doing that at some point." Phillip was gentle as he moved from behind me.

"Begging?" I liked the sound of that.

He was in view now. "Yes."

"But okay, you can watch. Only because you're pretty."

I raised my eyebrows at Dustin's words, unimpressed if he was teasing.

His smile was almost sheepish, and definitely adorable. "And smart. And sexy. And incredible."

"If you don't want to…" I let out a long sigh.

"He almost always wants to." Phillip grabbed the back of Dustin's neck and kissed him so hard I felt it in my teeth.

The give and take of watching them together was more arousing than any porn. It rivaled their touches on my own body. The give and take between them. Hard bodies pressed together and rough kisses exchanged as they stripped each other out of their clothes.

Being an observer let me appreciate the lines of muscle. The way they moved. The intensity that flowed between them and threatened to ignite the air around us.

Part of me wanted to tell them to slow down, so I could take longer to appreciate the experience, but I was too turned on and could tell they were too engrossed. Sparks and desire and need flowed from them.

My skin remembered their touches and those ghosts danced through me as I watched them with each other.

They broke apart long enough for Dustin to grab lube and condoms from the nightstand drawer.

They both rolled on protection and he handed Phillip the lube.

The lack of conversation and the seamless synchronicity of it all drove home how familiar this was to them, and somehow I was a part of it. I loved it.

Dustin crawled forward on the bed to kiss me. "Front row seats," he teased.

Phillip was generous with the lube, and as I watched him ease his way into Dustin from behind, I definitely wanted to get to a point where I could try that.

Phillip reached around to grab Dustin's cock, stroking as he pumped, slowly at first.

My arousal surged back as I watched them together. Apparently I wasn't completely spent. I teased myself as I watched them, trying to stay away from my clit for as long as I could.

Grunts, groans, and moans filled the air. The way Dustin held my gaze was hypnotic. Desire built inside me, surging and swelling.

The delicious sounds Dustin and Phillip made grew more stuttered. Phillip's hand dropped away and Dustin gripped his own shaft, balancing on one hand and stroking furiously with the other. His face screwed up and shudders rolled over him when he came.

God how was that so hot? At the sight, I couldn't hold back anymore. I focused in on the center of my need, circling my swollen clit, pushing myself until I reached climax again, waves crashing around and through me.

Phillip made those familiar noises that said he was close, and I swore I could feel when he paused, then slammed at a stuttered pace inside Dustin, finishing with a final, long grunt, before slowing to a stop.

None of us said much as they cleaned themselves and me up, then collapsed around me, propping me up between them and wrapping me in comfort and security and hugs.

"I really don't want to send you home in the morning." Dustin pressed his lips to my shoulder.

Me neither. "I don't quite know where *home* is right now. The apartment makes me uncomfortable." I felt bad that Cole did all that work to install the camera and everything, and I'd barely used it. He'd assured me that it was worth it, and that he'd already billed the apartment complex and encouraged them to contract with him to update every apartment.

"We can't leave you alone during the day," Phillip said.

Dustin nodded.

"I'm not an invalid. I have an arm I have to be careful with and believe me, it tells me when I'm not, and it's not my dominant arm."

"Still…" Phillip didn't sound convinced.

"Graham will let me stay with him as long as I need." It was a strange living arrangement, but it worked.

Dustin trailed his hand up my leg. "I want you after work every day. Both of you."

"I'm not a puppy you put in daycare until you're done with your day." My tone was light. I appreciated their concern, and I was a bit nervous about being on my own, despite my protests, or I'd be packing a bag now and seeing which of them was going to take me in.

"You are a kitty girl," Phillip pointed out.

"In game."

Dustin *tsk*ed. "You know how hard we've worked to make the game reflect reality."

I also knew that wasn't a valid argument. "All the way down to the magical railgun implants."

"We have time to figure it out." Phillip shifted so I could lay my head on his chest. "We have our entire lives ahead of us."

"Half our lives." Why did I feel it was necessary to point that out? Because I was me.

"Uh, no." Dustin almost sounded offended. "I'm going to live to be at least two-hundred."

"Complete with magical railgun implant?" Phillip teased.

Dustin shrugged. "Maybe. Hopefully."

I laughed at the exchange. I loved this part of our relationship too. I loved all of it.

"My *original* point"—the edge in Dustin's voice sounded exaggerated—"I'm going to want you both around as much as possible. Whether it's here or Phillip's, I don't care. And Adrienne, prepare to be smothered with overprotectiveness."

I smiled. "I never thought I'd be able to get into that, but it sounds wonderful."

Phillip stroked my hair back from my forehead to kiss me. "Good girl."

This was incredible. More amazing than I would've ever dared imagine for myself, and it was only going to get better from here.

epilogue

1 Year Later
    Phillip

Dustin and I stood on either side of the closed bathroom door, waiting impatiently. Adrienne was insistent that she loved us both, but no way was anyone watching her pee on a stick.

At the sound of the doorknob turning, I forced myself to breathe. Adrienne moved back to sit on the edge of the tub, pregnancy test in hand. "Now we wait for five minutes."

Right. Five minutes was nothing. Except we were five seconds in, and I already knew this would be the longest five minutes of my life since the last time I waited for pregnancy results.

Adrienne had been living here almost since we all exchanged *I love yous*, and early on she and I had an agreement—I'd get therapy for past trauma if she'd do the same. I'd insisted I was doing it for her, and confronting my grief had fucking *hurt*, but I was grateful both of us did it.

Healthier coping mechanisms didn't stop my memory from drifting toward having gone through this before, and from the vow I'd made that I'd never do it again.

That was before these two, though.

Dustin, Adrienne, and I had talked about this decision at length. About six months ago, about the time Dustin finally sold his house and moved in with us, we'd stopped using any sort of birth control. We didn't plan to see who the biological father was—Dustin and I would both be *Dad*.

But when Adrienne missed her period and had hints of morning sickness, I'd been struck with an ache of *familiar* that hadn't completely left.

Adrienne looked up. Five minutes already? One corner of her mouth tugged up, and the air was forced from my lungs in anticipation, despite knowing what she was about to say.

"It's positive." Disbelief and excitement buoyed her words.

My heart leaped into my throat.

Dustin let out a loud *whoop* and scooped Adrienne into his arms.

I'd never thought… I didn't…

"Are you all right?" Adrienne extracted herself from Dustin and rested a hand on my cheek. "Is this all right?"

At her touch and soft voice, my smile and relief surfaced. "This is better than all right." Joy and warmth flooded me. "This is incredible." I drew her into a tight embrace and brushed my lips over hers. "This is incredible. This is... *God*, I love you."

"I'm thinking mural in the baby's room," Dustin said.

"What kind of mural?" Adrienne pulled my arms around her and turned to face him, leaning into me. "No Aliens until they're old enough to ask for them."

Dustin stared at her in disbelief. "Give me some credit. I'm thinking water dragons and radish spirits and giant fluffy creatures."

"*Creatures* sounds dark." I was teasing. I had a feeling he meant more like cotton balls with feet.

"*Cute* creatures."

I laughed. Two years ago, I couldn't have imagined letting myself live through these experiences again, and now I couldn't imagine not having them. I was so grateful I hadn't let this pass me by. That Dustin and Adrienne hadn't let me pass them by.

Adrienne

When the doorbell rang, Dustin told me not to move, he had this. Phillip probably would have done the same, but he'd already decided I needed more herbal tea.

At five months pregnant, I was far from incapable of moving around the house, despite sometimes feeling I was waddling like a penguin, but they both pampered me and that was hard to complain about.

I heard Dustin answer the front door, and a chorus of voices drifted back.

A moment later, the patter of feet was accompanied by Phillip and Daria both calling, "No running in the house."

"*Addie.*" Harmony bounced onto the couch next to me and threw her arms around my neck. "Only four more months until the baby. Did you pick a name yet? I drew you a picture. Can I hang it in the baby's room? I—"

"Harmony, hon, you have to give her time to answer each question," Daria said from behind me.

"Okay." Harmony slid down the cushions and landed on her feet. "Where's your Christmas tree?"

Phillip set my tea on the coffee table and took the seat next to me. "In the basement. In its box."

Alana dropped into one of the chairs with a huff. "Not everyone puts their tree up early like a spaz."

Harmony mimicked the sound and crossed her arms. "Not everyone minds being a spaz."

They'd grown so much in just a year and a half, but they were still the same wonderful girls.

"We haven't put it up yet, because we need help." Dustin stopped next to Harmony. "You'd better be offering to help."

Alana rolled her eyes.

"Okay. Come on." Harmony grabbed Dustin's hand and tugged him toward the basement.

He glanced at Phillip. "I'm going to need help with the ornaments."

Phillip kissed me on the cheek before standing. "On it."

As the three of them headed downstairs, Daria settled next to me. "How are you holding up?"

"I've never had as many foot rubs in my entire life as in the last few months. Not that I'm complaining."

"Lucky bitch." Daria's tone was light. I adored her company. As far as sisters-in-law went, she was up there with Luna in terms of awesome—for different reasons—even if neither relationship was officially *by marriage*.

I grinned at the teasing. "I'll loan you Phillip for the day, if you need."

"Right. Like he's going to leave your side for more than five minutes anytime in the near future."

That was probably true.

"Where are we putting this?" Dustin's voice echoed from the stairwell.

Harmony ran into the room, a single box of ornaments in hand, and stopped in an empty corner near the fireplace. "This is where it went last year. It should go here again."

"Yes, ma'am." Dustin set about securing the artificial tree in place. "All yours."

Phillip set two large plastic storage boxes on the ground and opened both. "Make it pretty."

"Everyone has to help. Even Alana," Harmony announced. She skipped to the couch and grabbed both my hand and Daria's, and tugged.

A flutter moved through my belly, and I gasped, my hands flying to the sensation.

"Are you all right?" Phillip and Dustin asked at the same time.

I was glad they'd already put down what they were carrying. They were adorably attentive. "I'm fine," I assured them. "I think the baby's kicking."

Alana's eyes grew wide. "I wanna feel."

"Does it hurt?" Harmony sounded concerned.

"Okay, and no. Here." I grasped Harmony's hand and rested it on my stomach, where I'd felt the sensation. "Give it a minute."

Her face screwed up in intense focus. When another soft *thump* came from inside, she giggled. "It moved."

"My turn." Alana was insistent.

I let her rest her hand on my belly, too. At the next kick, her face lit up.

And then the expression vanished behind a blank mask. "When do you pull a Kane and it bursts from your stomach and gobbles faces?"

I swallowed a snort at the horrible visual, and Dustin winced.

"That doesn't happen, does it? That's not how babies are born." Now Harmony was horrified. "*Moooom*. Make her stop."

"No, that doesn't happen." Daria pulled Harmony into her lap, and glared at Dustin. "Alien? Really?"

Dustin shrugged. "She said you'd already let her see it. And I waited until Harmony went to bed." At least he had the sense to look sheepish.

Daria rolled her eyes, and set Harmony back on the ground. "Babies don't burst out of tummies like in the movie Alien. I promise. Addie will be fine. Go decorate the tree."

"Okay." Harmony ran back to the box of ornaments.

I joined in as we placed ornaments around the tree, trying to get at least half as many up high as Harmony hung on the bottom branches.

It was true that this wasn't my only family—my parents were wonderful, Graham and his partners were amazing, but this was different. This was a kind of closeness I couldn't have possibly have dreamed of a few years ago. When I was with Sean, especially after the cracks started to show in our relationship, I thought a life like this was out of my grasp.

I was so grateful it wasn't. This relationship, this reality, was the most incredible thing ever.

Dustin

I couldn't help but pace in the hospital waiting room. It wasn't fair that Phillip and I were out here, and Addie was in a delivery room by herself.

Okay, not technically *by herself*. She was surrounded by a doctor, nurses, an anesthesiologist... But we should be in there with her. We'd been told one of us could be during delivery.

The doctor had changed her mind after Addie went into labor, and kicked both Phillip and me out. The c-section was planned, but because the baby was breech, and other things the doctor saw that she wasn't sharing, there was a concern about complications and possibly needing general anesthesia.

Phillip was sitting in a chair, flipping through a magazine and pretending this didn't have him wound tighter than a spring. The fact that his leg hadn't stopped bouncing since he sat down indicated otherwise.

My internal scream escaped in a loud groan, and the couple of other people waiting on their own baby news shot me sympathetic looks.

I jumped, startled, when Phillip pressed into my back and wrapped his arms around my waist. "She's fine. *They'll* be fine. Better than fine."

You don't know that. I swallowed the retort—exactly the wrong thing to say, especially to him. "I know."

"I get it." He sighed and pressed his head to the back of mine.

I resigned myself to sitting and waiting, but I wasn't any more still than Phillip was.

When the doctor stepped into the waiting room, we were on our feet in an instant. She approached with a smile. As soon as she reached us, she said, "Both momma and baby are doing great. Fine and healthy."

My laugh of relief slipped out before I could stop it. I kept half an ear on the rest of what the doctor said—enough to pick up instructions and be reminded of what came next—but I was mostly waiting for her to say one thing.

"Would you like to meet your son?"

That was it.

Hours later—I wasn't paying attention to how much time had passed—I still couldn't get over how amazing this was. Addie was asleep in bed, looking as beautiful as I'd ever seen her. Phillip had gone to grab himself and me some food. And I was holding the baby. Again. This tiny little bundle of life nestled in my arms.

I'd been there when both of my nieces came home from the hospital, but this was different.

I cradled our baby, marveling at this tiny life we'd created. This sweet little soul we got to help grow up in this world.

Phillip returned, and set something pre-packaged on the table next to me. I looked at our baby boy, and then Phillip and Addie. This was nothing short of amazingly miraculous.

With the future stretching out in front of me—us—life had never been more incredible.

Thank you for reading Adrienne, Dustin, and Phillip's story. If you're looking for more Reese, Brandon, and Danny, they have their own tale in DUAL WIELDING.